BACK IN THE
LION'S DEN

BACK IN THE LION'S DEN

BY

ELIZABETH POWER

First published in Great Britain 2012
by Mills & Boon, an imprint of Harlequin (UK) Limited.
Large Print edition 2012
Harlequin (UK) Limited, Eton House,
18-24 Paradise Road, Richmond, Surrey TW9 1SR

© Elizabeth Power 2012

ISBN: 978 0 263 23640 8

Harlequin (UK) policy is to use papers that are natural, renewable and recyclable products and made from wood grown in sustainable forests. The logging and manufacturing process conform to the legal environmental regulations of the country of origin.

Printed and bound in Great Britain
by CPI Antony Rowe, Chippenham, Wiltshire

To Alan. With love always.

CHAPTER ONE

HE could hear the music coming from the fitness class before he reached it. A strong pulsing rhythm reverberating down the corridor.

On either side of him, behind glass partitions, enthusiasts were treading rubber and pumping muscle. He knew he cut an incongruous figure in his dark business suit, white shirt and tie, and was aware that two young women playing squash on one of the courts he was passing had stopped their game to watch him.

At six feet three and powerfully built, with the sleek black hair and rugged features of a Celtic heritage, he was used to the attention his presence elicited from the opposite sex. But while he might usually have spared a glance towards an admiring female today Conan Ryder's mind wasn't distracted from its purpose.

Ignoring their blatant interest, he strode determinedly on, the green-gold of his eyes remaining focused on the partly open door to the room where the beat was coming from. His broad shoulders were pulled back in a deliberate attempt to stem the adrenalin that was coursing through his body.

No one made him feel like this! The fight for the composure he prized pulled his jaw into a grim cast. Especially not a woman—and particularly not a woman like Sienna Ryder! He had a request to make—that was all. A request she'd probably refuse so that would mean a verbal battle with her to get her to do what he wanted. But he would win in the end. After that it was a matter of making the necessary arrangements and getting out.

'That's good, Charlene! Let your hips do the work! That's lovely! You're a natural! Let it f-l-o-w…'

He heard her voice above the beat as he pushed open the door with the flat of his hand. Clear. Encouraging. In control.

The lively rhythm was still pounding as he met the class head on and twenty pairs of female eyes turned his way, but his interest lay only with the petite figure of the young woman in a sleeveless red leotard and black leggings who was still directing the class with her back to him.

Her short dark hair was expertly shaped into the nape of her neck, its boyish style only adding to her femininity. Skin lightly tanned, the perfect proportions of her small, slim body were clearly outlined by the clinging clothes, yet there was a remarkably lithe fitness about her that hadn't been so apparent when she had been married to his brother.

Coming up behind her, he let his gaze sweep over the graceful line of her neck and shoulders to the small butterfly tattoo he recognised just above her right shoulderblade, and felt a tug of unwelcome awareness at the very core of his masculinity. He found himself having to clear his throat before he stooped to make himself heard.

'I'm sorry to interrupt your workout, but you were proving far too elusive. How does anyone get in touch with you? By carrier pigeon?' Past hostilities gave a hard edge to the deep resonance of his voice. 'Or would I have had more luck trying telepathy?'

Shock had registered in her eyes as she'd swung round—big blue eyes that met the green-gold of his now with a spark of contention, acknowledging the coldness in his tones.

'Hello, Conan.' Her smile was bright and forced, her small oval face assuming that look of cool detachment he remembered so well. 'It's lovely to see you again too.'

Her sarcasm wasn't lost on him, but then he saw the blood drain from her cheeks as she said starkly, 'Daisy? Is she all right?'

Her concern for her child was obvious, even if she hadn't shown the same regard for his brother.

'How would I know?' he lobbed back across the fading beat. 'I haven't seen her in nearly three years!' Censure stiffening every inch of his strong, lean body, he watched her dark lashes come down as that moment of panic gave way to undisguised relief as it dawned on her that he couldn't possibly know anything about the welfare of his niece. 'I've been trying to reach you for days, but your landline's ex-directory, and each time I've called at the house you've never been around.'

She looked almost startled. Perhaps she had never expected him to find out where she lived. 'We've been busy.' It was a flat refusal to enlarge upon anything concerning her private life. 'Why did you want to see me anyway?'

Tension pulled in his jaw at the rising level of female hormones in the hall. Now that the music had stopped he could feel those twenty pairs of eyes looking him up and down, as though they had never seen a man before in their entire lives.

Impatiently he demanded, 'Can we talk somewhere else?'

Gesturing for her class to continue as another track started to play, Sienna simply jerked her head towards the open door.

Reaching it first, Conan caught the scent of the freshness of her skin as she stepped past him into the corridor. He noticed the sway of her slim hips as he followed her out, and with another stab of something way down in his loins noticed the shape of her firm buttocks, tantalisingly separated by the deep lines of the leotard, the narrow span of her waist as she went ahead of him with her head high, her back as proud and straight as any ballerina's.

'What do you want?' she challenged, swinging to face him.

Her blood was racing just at the sight of seeing Conan Ryder on her turf. He was as hard and handsome as she remembered him. Business entrepreneur. Billionaire. And her late husband's half-brother.

He was right, though. It *had* been three years—or as good as—since she had fled from Surrey to her home town just outside London, escaping his cruel taunts and his accusations with an eighteen month old toddler in tow. Three years since that tragic accident of Niall's that had left her widowed and her child fatherless.

It was clear from Conan's disparaging manner that his opinion of her hadn't changed. Now, alone with him, she felt less like the confident, self-sufficient woman she had become, and more like the emotionally dependent girl who had taken the lash of his tongue with no means of defending herself. Nothing that would explain her actions, why she had lied, her obvious guilt. Not without baring her very soul to him, and there was no way she was ever going to do that.

Closing her mind against the bitter pain that threatened to well up inside of her, she murmured in a voice that was near to cracking, 'For what reason could you possibly want to see me?'

'Not you.' Those incisive words cut across her with the precision of a scythe. 'Daisy. I'm here to insist you let Daisy come back with me.'

'What?' Her stomach muscles tightened at painful echoes of the past. *'I'd do everything in my power to take Daisy away from you.'* Yet her hackles were rising too, at the sheer arrogance of his statement, making her respond with, 'Insist? You *insist,* Conan?'

'She's my brother's child,' he reminded her harshly. 'She also has a grandmother she hasn't seen.'

'She also has a mother who wasn't good enough for any of you—remember?' It was a pointed little cry. Poignant, bitter and accusing.

Conan's black lashes swept down over the glittering green of his eyes—thick long lashes, she'd always thought, that most women would give their eye teeth to achieve. His face was lean and hard, high cheekbones stark against the proud nostrils that flared momentarily above his angular, darkly shadowed jaw, and the taut line of his wide, uncompromising mouth was compressed.

'All right,' he breathed heavily at length. 'I know we've had our differences.'

'Our differences?' She almost laughed in his face. 'Is that what you call them, Conan? Being accused of being an unfit mother and an unfaithful wife?'

His penetrating eyes hardened like chips of green glass, but all he said was, 'Yes, well…' It was clear he didn't want to discuss the accusations he had made. 'That doesn't alter the fact that you had no right to deprive Daisy of her family.'

'I had every right!' The star-shaped studs in her ears glinted as she brought her head up sharply, colour touching her cheeks at his glaring audacity. A confrontation with him was bad enough, but being so scantily dressed made her feel at even more of a disadvantage—especially since he was so big and so potently male. 'Niall was all the family she had. Niall and me!' That wasn't strictly true, Sienna thought, because there were her parents, although she didn't see them that often since their move to Spain.

'Niall was my brother.'

'Yes, well…a pity you didn't remember that when he was alive!'

She had hit a raw nerve. She could see it in the way that sensuous mouth of his hardened, and in the way his irises seemed to darken like woodland pools at dusk. Perhaps being reminded of how he, a self-made billionaire, had refused his own brother help when he'd been in desperate financial straits didn't sit too comfortably on his conscience. With lethal softness, however, he said, 'You still want to goad me with that?'

Something warned her to be on her guard and not to antagonise him unnecessarily. Even so, the raw pain to which he had subjected her three years ago, with his implacable assumptions and his inexorably cruel accusations, had her uttering tautly, 'I don't want to do *anything* with you, Conan Ryder.'

His gaze grazed over her shoulders, touching briefly on the swell of her small firm breasts. He was unpitying and unscrupulous and she didn't like him, and yet she felt the sick stirrings of a ridiculous heat lick along her veins.

'Did I ever ask you to?' he enquired silkily, the

cruel mockery that played around his mouth leaving her in no doubt as to what he meant.

No, he hadn't, she thought with an inexplicable little tingle along her spine, and she had never thought of him as anything other than her husband's elder brother. Of course she'd been aware of his countless attributes during those two and a half years she had been married to Niall. What woman wouldn't have been? she reasoned resentfully. He was good-looking, dynamic, and unbelievably wealthy. He was also a dark and silent entity she'd never quite been able to fathom out, although his ruthlessness and insensitivity had been all too apparent at the end. She would have had to be an android not to have *noticed* him, at least. But she'd loved Niall. Loved him with a passion that had nearly driven her insane...

'If I remember correctly,' he was saying icily now, 'you were too busy breaking your marriage vows without any help from me—though I doubt it would have taken much more than a snap of my fingers, even with your lover in the picture.'

'He wasn't my lover! And you're still as misguided as you ever were if you think I would ever have thought about setting my sights on a man like *you!*' Memories of the last time she had stood and faced him like this clawed at her consciousness, the ugly scene forever etched on her memory. 'For your information, Conan—'

I loved your brother, she had been about to say, but broke off as the door to her gym class opened, enveloping them in a pounding rhythm.

A young woman came out, her smile for Conan openly inviting before she crossed behind him to the women's cloakroom, forcing him to move closer to Sienna.

In her tight, revealing clothes she suddenly felt naked beside him, and the air left her lungs so that it felt difficult to breathe.

This close to him she could smell the lemony fragrance of his cologne. It didn't help either that he was so formally dressed, probably having just come from some high-flying meeting, she guessed grudgingly, where he'd made multi-million-pound decisions that would increase his global fortune tenfold! But his nearness was stifling, and Sienna took a step back—which was so obvious that he couldn't have failed to realise why.

Apart from the lift of an enquiring eyebrow, however, fortunately he made no comment.

'My mother needs to see Daisy,' he stated as the cloakroom door closed quietly behind him. 'So do I.' Sombre lines were etched around his mouth and jaw and a deep groove corrugated the healthily tanned skin of his forehead. 'My mother hasn't been herself lately...' He couldn't bring himself to tell her what was really wrong, how worried he was about Avril Ryder; he wasn't going to beg. 'And I feel she would benefit from a visit from her only grandchild. She hasn't seen her since she was eighteen months old. Neither of us has.'

'And you think you can just come here and take Daisy away? Just like that? That I'd even allow it?' Fear rose in her again but she forced it back. 'She doesn't know you, Conan.'

'And whose fault is that?'

'She doesn't know you,' she reiterated, ignoring his censuring demand. 'Neither of us does.' Or did, she amended bitterly, reminded of his heartlessness, his lack of compassion—not just towards her, but towards his own brother.

'I'm the child's uncle, for Pete's sake! Not that you've ever given her the chance to find out. There have been no photos. No contact. Do you know what that's been like for Avril? Her *grandmother*? Don't you think she's had enough to contend with in losing Niall—without losing his baby daughter as well when you took her away?'

'I was driven away,' she breathed fiercely. 'And you seem to forget...I lost something too.' Her eyes were shielded, their lids heavy with the pain of remembering. 'I lost a husband. And I had to contend with a lot of accusations and blame. Don't you think I felt bad enough without being made to feel I was responsible for what had happened to him? That I was responsible for his drinking and getting into debt? I knew what you thought of me—both of you. You made it clear often enough that you thought Niall had married beneath him.'

'I've never said that.'

'You didn't have to! It was there in every last criticism of everything I said—everything I did. Your mother could scarcely contain her shock at him marrying a barmaid! Albeit a temporary one, until I could get my career on track! But that was the crux of the matter, wasn't it? You were determined not to like me from the start.'

'I'm not responsible for my mother. As for me, I only acted on what I observed with my own eyes.'

'And what was that? Besides my supposed infidelity, that is?'

Condemnation set his features in harsh lines, so that he looked like one of the warring Celts whose blood still pumped through his proud, pulsing veins. 'You know very well. Niall was weak where money was concerned. He was living above his means and you did nothing but encourage him.'

Because she hadn't known. Because she'd been

too young to recognise the signs: his irritability, his drinking too much, his mood swings.

'"Bled him dry",' she reminded him. 'That was the phrase I believe you used.'

He didn't negate or deny it. How could he? Sienna thought grimly. He wasn't a man to pull his punches, or hide behind lies and subterfuge—as she had—whatever else he might have done.

'I can't talk about this now,' she uttered quickly, hearing the last track on the album she'd selected earlier come to an abrupt end. 'I've got to get back to my class.' This meeting with Niall's brother was more traumatic than she'd ever have imagined possible, and it was with aching relief that she pulled herself away.

'You'll do as I ask, Sienna.'

She stopped in her tracks, swinging round to face him again, her eyes wide with defiance and disbelief.

'Oh, will I? And what do you intend to do to try and bully me into it? Concoct some tale about my being an unsuitable mother and get an injunction to try and take Daisy away from me, as you threatened before?' Beneath her bravado was a sick anxiety that he might try to do just that—somehow use his power and influence to get even with her for how he believed she had treated Niall.

'I didn't come here for that.'

'No. You just want me to hand her over without all the hassle. Well, I'm sorry, Conan, but the answer's still no. Daisy's not going anywhere without me, and I'm certainly not putting myself back into the lion's den, thank you very much!'

'Oh, I think you will, Sienna.'

'And what makes you so sure?'

'Conscience, sweetheart. If you have one.'

Her small chin came up as she said bitterly, ignoring the patronising way in which he had addressed her, 'Like you, you mean?'

She didn't wait to catch any sniping response.

Making sure Daisy was asleep, Sienna kissed the little girl's soft cheek before extinguishing her bedside lamp, unable to resist stroking the silky chestnut hair that curled against the pillow.

Like Niall's, she thought poignantly, pulling the duvet up over the chubby arm wrapped around her pink hippopotamus. Daisy had inherited her father's colouring, not hers.

Going back downstairs, she opened the back door to let in a big bouncing bundle of white shaggy fur, filled a bowl with the dog's supper, and then started the ironing—normal things she did every day, except tonight things felt anything but normal.

Meeting Conan again had opened up all the unhappiness of the past, forcing her to dwell on wounds she'd thought had healed, forcing her to think, to remember.

She had been just twenty when she had met Niall.

With her parents having sold their UK home to live abroad, Sienna had chosen to stay in England on her own. Her parents had always done their own thing. They liked sun, sea and sand, and Sienna had been happy for them, while relishing the prospect of occasional holidays in Spain.

She had been working as a receptionist at her local gym when she had met Niall. He had been a regular member there, and had often come into the bar where she had sometimes helped when it was short-staffed. She had instantly warmed to his wicked sense of humour. He'd been witty and charming, and just a little bit crazy, and she'd been swept off her feet before she had known what hit her.

Her parents had flown over for the wedding, which had been a short civil ceremony after a whirlwind romance. Faith and Barry Swann and Niall's mother—a barrister's widow—were poles apart, and while they'd tried to befriend her new mother-in-law it was clear that Avril Ryder hadn't really warmed towards them. It had also been clear to Sienna from the start that the woman believed she had trapped her youngest son into marriage by getting pregnant, which was something over which Sienna had been silently smug, proving her wrong when Daisy had arrived exactly a year to the day that they had married.

Conan had been at the wedding, interrupting some important business conference he'd been attending in Europe, and the cool touch of his lips on her cheek as he'd wished her well after the ceremony had been as formal as it had been unsettling.

It had been clear, though, that Niall looked up to his brother, and Sienna had understood why. Already approaching his late twenties to his half-brother's twenty-three, and spearheading a global telecommunications company, Conan Ryder had been a mind-blowing success—dynamic, wealthy and sophisticated. It had been apparent to Sienna from the start who Niall was trying to emulate in the way he spoke, in his image, even in that air of glacial composure that Conan exuded.

Niall had been a top sales executive working at Conan's head office, though not before pulling himself out of university and destroying his mother's hopes of him following his late father into the legal profession. Nevertheless, he had been good at his job, and determined that she would reap the benefits—from the clothes he had bought her to every conceivable luxury she had wanted in their modern four bedroom home, a house he had mortgaged only a few miles from his half-brother's Surrey mansion.

But he'd played as hard as he worked. Often too hard, Sienna remembered painfully, as she ironed the back of one of Daisy's little blouses for at least the third time. Because it had been that reckless sense of fun and that daredevil attitude towards almost everything that had killed him during those five days in Copenhagen at that stag party that had gone terribly wrong…

Pain and remorse pressed like twin bars against her chest, and she forced herself to breathe deeply to ease the anguish.

While he'd been alive he'd been driven: always trying to compete—almost obsessively so, she reflected—with his elder brother. But Niall hadn't had Conan's focus—or his ruthlessness, she thought bitterly. Because when Niall had got into dire financial straits and had asked his brother for help, just a couple of weeks before he'd died, Conan had refused. Niall had been devastated. It was only then that he'd told her how far they had been living above their means and just how much money they owed. She'd been too young and far too naive to realise it!

Both Conan and her mother-in-law had blamed *her* for her husband's overspending, and for the worry she had caused, which had led to his drinking and his ultimate accident.

'It wasn't my fault!' she'd shot back at Conan that last day, just a week after Niall's funeral, hurting, agonised, reproaching herself for going along with everything Niall had expected of her—given her—even when her instincts had told her that he was wrong, or that it seemed he was being far too extravagant. 'And if *you'd* helped him when he came to you for help perhaps he wouldn't have got so drunk as not to know what he was doing!' she had flung at him bitterly, too overcome by grief to care what she was saying.

She had wanted desperately to cry. To break down. To alleviate the pain pressing like a dead weight against her chest. But standing there in the sumptuous drawing room of Conan Ryder's Regency home, where she'd come to return the last of Niall's things, her tears wouldn't come. She had felt only a numbing emptiness that had given her an air of spurious indifference—which had only cemented her guilt in his brother's eyes, promoting what he'd decided he already knew: that she'd been cheating on his brother.

'My brother was in trouble and you weren't even aware of it—too wrapped up in your spending and your...*boyfriend* to notice.'

'Oh, I noticed all right!' It was a bitter little cry, torn from beneath the veneer of icy detachment she was feeling.

'And you did nothing to help him.'

'I was his wife—not his nursemaid!' She realised how cold and brutal that sounded. She was trying to defend herself and failing miserably, wanting to scream at Niall for leaving her to face his family like this—alone. Hurt, angry, reproaching herself...

'My mother has expressed concerns that you aren't mature or responsible enough to look after a child—and quite frankly I agree with her. I want my brother's offspring to grow up as a Ryder, under this family's roof. Not in some other man's home, bearing some other man's name.'

'She'll grow up as I consider fit,' she assured him, stung by the things her mother-in-law had said. But then Avril Ryder—whom, she noted, hadn't emerged from her own wing of her eldest son's exclusive residence—had never made any attempt to conceal her disapproval of her other son's match. There was no way, though, that Sienna ever intended changing her child's name—even if she did end up with another man in the far distant future. 'You're not her father, Conan,' she reminded him coolly. 'Even if you'd like to think you are.'

'No.' Derision curved his uncompromising mouth at that. 'Fortunately I can't claim to be among those to have had the pleasure.'

Her hand clenched with the almost uncontrollable urge to lash out at him, to feel the sting of her palm as it met the hardness of his cheek which might shake her out of this numbing misery. But she'd decided that enough damage had been done already.

'I don't have to stay here and take this from you,' she responded quietly, hating herself for the tingle of awareness that had run through her at his blatant innuendo a moment ago. 'But if you're trying to make me feel cheap, then go ahead. I was never good enough for you, was I? *Either* of you,' she'd added accusingly. 'Is that why Niall made such a mess of things? Because he was made to feel he wasn't good enough either? Because he felt so overshadowed by his much smarter, richer and generally more favoured elder brother?'

If he'd looked angry before, he'd looked livid

then, his proud nostrils flaring, the skin above his upper lip white with rage. 'You don't know what you're talking about,' he'd rasped.

'Don't I?' She went on goading him, unable to help herself, needing something—anything—to ease the burden of confusing emotions that were ravaging her. 'I know you did next to nothing to support him—in *anything*—and that when he came to you for help you refused him any financial backing! Well, don't worry! We'll be leaving tomorrow. You won't have to put up with me soiling this family's precious pedigree any more!'

'You take Daisy away from here and you'll have me to answer to. Is that clear?'

'As crystal! What do you propose to do?' she taunted. 'Sue for custody?'

'If it comes to it.'

'On what grounds?' she challenged, suddenly wary. 'That I'm an unfit mother?' Painfully she remembered the instances that had helped tar her with that particular brush—the circumstances that she couldn't explain even if she wanted to.

'If I find you wanting in that regard, I won't hesitate in applying for Daisy to be made a ward of court, most certainly.'

From anyone else she would have considered it

an idle threat. From Conan it merely struck the deepest fear into her heart.

He was rich and powerful enough to make any court take notice of charges he made against her. And though she doubted that the Ryders would ever be allowed full custody of her daughter, she still feared what he might try to do with his staggering influence and his money.

'Well, perhaps I should marry my *boyfriend!*' she threw back desperately, pandering to his previous accusation. 'And then you wouldn't be able to do a thing! Stay away from me, Conan!'

She'd stormed out of the house and their lives without another glance back, paying off her debts and setting up home in the little terraced house she'd managed to mortgage with the small amount of capital left over from the sale of the house she had shared with Niall.

But now Conan had turned up again, still as judgmental as ever, and with a lethal maturity only acquired by three more years of honing that indomitable strength of character alongside his superb masculine physique. Of increasing his wealth and power and making himself one of the most talked about entrepreneurs of his generation—both in the playgrounds of the rich and in his corporate life. It amounted to three more years of getting what he wanted. And he wanted Daisy...

When the doorbell rang, she almost dropped the iron.

CHAPTER TWO

SHADOW—so named because of the patch of black fur covering the whole of one side of his head and one floppy ear—was barking frantically at the front door by the time Sienna reached it.

'Conan!' She didn't know why she sounded surprised. She had known he would come.

The dog was leaping excitedly up at him, with no regard for his designer tailoring, while Conan, with a face like granite, stood rigidly impervious, his nostrils flaring and his olive skin infused with something almost akin to anger.

'I'm sorry. He isn't usually like this,' Sienna apologised, rushing forward to grab the dog's collar. In fact, after bringing the six month old Shadow home from an animal rescue centre two years ago, she had been pleased when her pet had flown through obedience classes with the equivalent of a doggy distinction. Rather grudgingly though she decided that just the mere sight of a man like Conan Ryder was enough to make even a mere animal forget its manners.

'May I come in?'

With every nerve on alert, still holding the dog's collar, Sienna backed away to admit him.

Immediately the walls of the narrow passageway seemed to close in on all sides, the space between them shrunk by his imposing physique.

With a tightness in her chest, Sienna took another step back for an entirely different reason, releasing the dog which, after one brave sniff at the man's black designer shoes, trotted off to the comfort of the living room.

Her mouth dry, Sienna demanded, 'What's this all about, Conan? Because if it's about Daisy you've had a wasted journey. I thought I made my position clear this afternoon.'

For a split second something flared in his eyes. Anger? Retaliation? She wasn't sure. But with that strong self-command she had always envied about him he brought it under control, only the muscle that pulled in his darkly shadowed jaw disclosing any other sign of emotion.

'We parted on a rather bad note today. I thought it only right to try and rectify that.'

Oh, did you?

His dark head tilted towards the door at the end

of the passageway, his meaning obvious, while an arresting movement of his devastating mouth caused a peculiar flutter in the pit of her stomach.

Conan Ryder being hostile was something she could deal with. Conan being charming was far more dangerous to her equilibrium.

'You'd better come through.' She wondered if he had detected that nervous note in her voice, and as she went ahead of him along the passageway could almost feel his eyes boring through her tight black T-shirt and jeans.

Too aware of him as she led him into her tiny sitting room, she sensed his brooding gaze moving critically over its rather jaded décor. 'Sit down.' She looked around the cramped little room in dismay. 'If you can find a space.' She darted to remove the pile of ironing from her one easy chair, dragging toys and a jigsaw puzzle box off the worn, rather lumpy-looking settee beside it.

Ignoring her, he was looking around at the rather shabby and tired-looking furnishings, the few sparse pieces of furniture that made up a wooden table and chairs, a rather stressed bookcase, a modest hi-fi system and her television.

'Is this how you're living?' Censure marked the hard lines of his face.

Eyeing him resentfully, with a pile of freshly

ironed garments supported on her hip, Sienna snapped, 'What's that supposed to mean?'

Conan's mouth pulled down hard on one side. 'A bit of a change, isn't it, from what you were used to?'

'At least it's all paid for!' It was an anguished throwback to the girl who had blindly accepted every luxury without question—only to find herself plunged into widowhood with nothing but loneliness, a precious little toddler and a whole heap of debt.

'With what?' Derision laced Conan's voice as he sliced another detrimental glance around the sad little living space, finishing up on Shadow who was gazing up at him from his shabbily cushioned basket with suspicious eyes. 'You can scarcely earn much from that menial job you do at that gym.'

'And what's it to you?' She hadn't meant to snap. He'd come to try and patch things up, after all. But his criticism of her home and his disparaging reference to what she did when she had trained so hard—worked so hard—to keep a roof over her and Daisy's head was proving more than she could take.

'Everything—if I think my niece is being deprived of the most essential necessities when she could be benefiting from the help that her mother is too proud—or to selfish—even to consider.'

Sienna's hackles rose—not least because she *was* sometimes worried that her daughter was missing out on some of the things her little friends obviously enjoyed. Like bouncy castles on her birthday and pretty clothes; like the reliability of a car that wasn't breaking down every five minutes. Like a father who hadn't died and left her...

Regret mingled with anger—the anger she often reproached herself for feeling towards Niall and the way he had died when it had all been so avoidable. So pointless...

'Proud and selfish you might think me,' she quoted, pulling herself up to her full five feet four inches to face Niall's brother with a display of composure she was far from feeling, 'and perhaps I am. But as far as what I said to you three years ago, when you very kindly condescended to offer us financial assistance goes...' Her voice dripped pure venom. 'I don't retract a single word.'

The animosity she felt towards him lay thickly on the air between them. Conan felt it like a live thing, along with the silent, anguished accusation that rose like a torturing spectre from the darkest recesses of his mind.

You didn't want to help us when Niall was alive! We can do without any help from you now!

Heavily, with some private emotion seeming to stretch the skin taut across his prominent cheekbones, he pointed out, 'Even if Daisy suffers because of it?'

'She won't,' Sienna returned, with more conviction than she was feeling, glancing down at Shadow, who was making rather indelicate grunting noises as he delved violently into his fur.

'Then at least allow her to see her grandmother.' His denigrating glance towards the basket told her he probably didn't approve of her dog either. 'You have a duty, Sienna. To Niall's family as well as your own.'

'Duty?' She almost laughed in his face. What right had he to talk about *duty* when he had never really cared about his half-brother? When he had turned his back on him when Niall had needed him most? 'He never asked you for anything,' she accused bitterly, wanting to drive away memories that were too painful to remember. 'When he did...' She had to swallow to continue. 'He looked up to you and he needed you. He was desperate,' she muttered, 'and you just weren't there for him.'

'And you think *I* killed him? Drove him to drink so much that he overbalanced on that bridge when he took up his friends' ridiculous challenge to walk along that wall? Isn't that what you said?'

There was raw emotion in his voice—in the perfect structure of his hard-hewn features. Had he loved his brother after all? Despite everything? Or was it just a pricking of his conscience that was responsible for the darkening of his amazing eyes.

'I didn't know what I was saying.' Vainly she strove to redress the situation, to justify what she had thoughtlessly flung at him because of his accusations. If he'd loved Niall half as much as she had they would have lain heavily—would still lie heavily—on his conscience. 'As I said earlier—I'd just lost my husband.'

'And I'd lost a brother.'

She was right. Her words had left an indelible mark on him. She could see it—hear it in the dark resonant depths of his voice.

For a moment they faced each other like warring combatants—Sienna with her cheeks flushed, eyes glittering defensively, Conan's olive features tinged with angry colour.

He was every bit the Celt, Sienna decided distractedly, from his thick black hair to his strong, proud Gaelic bone structure. In his pride and in his daunting self-sufficiency. In that unmistakable air of command that surrounded him, which made him lead where other men could merely follow. Both brothers had been handsome men. Niall had had the cheek and the charm of his mother's Celtic bloodline, but it was Conan who bore his Irish ancestry like a blazing flag.

'My mother's unwell,' he stated, quietly and succinctly. 'She's very unwell.' In fact the doctors had told him that Avril Ryder didn't seem to have the will to recover. The dark fringes of his lashes came down to veil his eyes. 'I've brought her to stay with me in France.' He owned a spectacular villa these days on the Côte d'Azur, Sienna remembered from an article she had read about him. 'She needs cheering up, and I know her greatest wish is to see her only grandchild. You will come with Daisy, of course—I wouldn't expect anything else—and with the holidays coming up, I'll expect you to stay for the summer.'

A strong refusal sprang to Sienna's lips—but she couldn't express it. If the Ryders—Conan especially—only wanted to salve their consciences by making up for lost time with Daisy, that was one thing. They could go whistle for all she cared. But from the look on his face as he'd told her about his mother things sounded pretty serious. What if this was the last chance Daisy might have of seeing her grandmother? Sienna found herself considering reluctantly. Wouldn't she be doing her daughter a grave injustice by refusing to let her go? And if Avril Ryder *was* that sick...

The holidays *were* coming up, as he had said and her regular classes were coming to an end. She found herself assessing the matter before she had fully realised it. She did have individual training sessions to honour. Also, she couldn't afford to take that much time off without it eating severely into her already frugal budget. But if she did give in and condescend to grant his wishes, she'd be darned if she'd let Daisy go anywhere—or *stay* anywhere—without her!

'I—I can't take that much time off,' she found herself eventually admitting hesitantly. Though her ethics might be forcing her to do what anyone with half a conscience would do, she didn't want to suffer the indignity of Niall's brother guessing just how little money she had, or just how hard she was struggling to make ends meet. 'I would if I could, but I can't.'

Conan's eyes moved reflectively over her pleasingly toned and agile figure.

Of course, he thought, with an introspective smile touching the firm line of his mouth. He'd guessed she could use her job as an excuse. But women like her could be bought—for a price. Hadn't he seen evidence of it in the luxuries she had demanded from her husband? In the clothes and the designer jewellery? In the fast car she'd been happy to buy out of his limited funds before she'd found herself more interesting fish to fry?

'Wives don't come cheap, bruv...as you've yet to find out.' Across the years he heard his late brother's almost bragging statement after he'd warned Niall about his spending, and remembered, some time later, accusing Sienna of taking his brother for every penny she could get.

'I will pay you what you earn—I'll triple it,' he assured her coldly. The reminder of the type of woman she was had turned his heart to stone.

Now, why didn't that offer surprise her? she thought grimly.

'That's very generous of you.' Sienna gave him a bright, unfaltering smile. 'But can you safeguard my position until I come back?'

'If I have to.'

Of course. The Conan Ryders of this world could get anything they wanted. They snapped their fingers and lesser mortals jumped to do their bidding. How stupid of her even to ask!

'I take it, then, that that's a yes?' he pressed.

She didn't answer, deciding to wait to tell him that if she did agree to what he wanted she had no intention of taking a penny of his precious money. Why spoil his mean and miserable opinion of her? she thought, following his gaze to where it was resting on Shadow, who was making violent sucking noises now as he burrowed with increasing ferocity into his fur.

'Does that dog of yours have a problem with ticks?'

'No, he doesn't!' What *was* the emotion that was turning down the corners of his superbly masculine mouth? she wondered. Disapproval? Dislike? And why was she even *looking* at his mouth? she thought, annoyed with herself. Let alone considering it superb?

Refraining from telling him that Shadow's problem sprang from rolling on a chocolate wrapper while on his walk this evening, much to the surprise and angry retaliation of a few disgruntled wasps, she enquired breezily, 'Don't you like dogs?'

A broad shoulder lifted beneath the tailored jacket. 'I can take them or leave them. Let's just say I wouldn't choose to share my home with one.'

Well, tough! Sienna thought, but said brightly,

and with some relish, 'That's all right, then. Because if you want to take Daisy and me away with you for the summer I'm afraid you're going to have to take us all.'

'I thought you said Conan never had much time for his brother?' Faith Swann commented when Sienna rang her parents to tell them where she would be going and why. 'That he was positively heartless towards him, and that Avril Ryder was always making you feel inferior and criticising the way you were bringing up my granddaughter?' Faith was fiercely protective of those she loved, and was constantly trying to persuade Sienna to bring Daisy to join her and her husband in Spain.

'He was—and she was,' Sienna averred, and though she hated having to acknowledge it she said, sighing, 'But they're Daisy's family too. And no matter how they treated me, or Niall, as his mother's not well I have to go.'

'I expect he can be quite persuasive,' her mother was remarking distractedly about her late son-in-law's brother. 'I only saw him in the flesh that once...' She meant at the wedding. 'But I saw a picture of him recently in one of our English news-papers,' Faith continued. 'He's quite a looker, isn't he? Not so obviously handsome as Niall was, but the more moody and magnificent type that a lot of women go for. At least he *looked* moody in that photograph,' she added with a little chuckle. 'Probably because he was caught hurrying from the executive lounge of some airport with his latest adoring companion. You know that chat show hostess? Petra Somebody-or-other?'

'Petra Flax,' Sienna supplied, not unfamiliar with the raven-haired beauty whose twice-weekly programme was a little too gossipy for her own taste.

'Just wait until I tell the regulars and our friends at the golf club that my daughter's hobnobbing with the likes of Conan Ryder.'

'Mum!' Sienna burst out, cringing at her mother's penchant for dropping names—the more influential the better. 'I'd appreciate it if you didn't.'

'Don't be silly,' Faith remonstrated, having clearly lapped up the news that Sienna was going to be in the bosom of her late husband's family. 'I'm proud that my daughter had the good sense to marry a man with such illustrious connections. So should you be.'

'Yes, Mum.' Sienna sighed resignedly, reminded of how much her mother enjoyed basking in other people's reflected glory, and remembering that it was those very traits of Faith Swann's that had gone a long way to letting Sienna and her family down with Avril Ryder and her friends on that one inauspicious occasion when their families had met.

'Don't take any notice of your mother. She means well,' Barry Swann placated, when he came on the line to talk to his daughter. 'I know you've always liked to play things close to your chest, but just remember we're here, love, if you need us. For anything at all.'

Strangely, that simple token of kindness from her father produced a welling of emotion in Sienna.

She'd never worried her parents with the reason for her estrangement from Niall's family, or with the extent of Conan's accusations—that he'd not only as good as accused her of being a gold-digger, but also of cheating on his brother. If she had, her father would have come over here to sort him out, she thought sadly, yet with a wry grimace, because she didn't give much for the chances of anyone who tried locking horns with Conan Ryder.

And anyway, what could she tell them? That Conan was right? That the morning he'd come looking for her to tell her that her husband had died he'd discovered she'd spent the night in another man's flat.

She shuddered at the prospect of all the hurt and anger that would follow if she did disclose the truth to them. She couldn't. Wouldn't! she vowed grittily, aching under the weight of it.

'Thanks, Dad,' she murmured gratefully, and rang off.

'So who's this guy you're going to be spending the summer with?' Jodie Fisher asked as Sienna, returning from some last minute shopping before Conan arrived to pick them up, joined her on her porch after locking up her clapped out little red saloon.

'He's my brother-in-law—and I'm not spending the summer with *him,* as such,' she corrected, keen to dispel any hopes her neighbour—a wild-haired blonde, who was noticeably pregnant and the mother of a four-year old—might be harbouring about her having designs on any man…least of all Conan Ryder. 'Well I am, but not in the way you think. My mother-in-law's sick,' she outlined, feeling a nagging unease about how the woman would receive her. She didn't elaborate to Jodie. Although Jodie was a good friend, often looking after Daisy at a moment's notice—as she had done today—Sienna hadn't confided to her exactly what the situation was with her late husband's family. Such things were private. She had simply told

Jodie that they lived miles away and she didn't see them very often.

'You wouldn't be lying to me now, would you?' Jodie's attention was caught by something over Sienna's shoulder. 'Great Jumping Jacks! Wowee! Is that a BMW? Or is *that* a BMW? Is that *him?* No, don't tell me! Let me guess! He's pulling in here. It's him! What I wouldn't give for a brother-in-law who looked like that!'

Jodie was clearly knocked sideways. But why the man made every woman who cast eyes on him want to swoon at his feet was beyond her, Sienna though grudgingly, with a careless glance over her shoulder. Yet the dark magnetism of the man behind the wheel of the graphite grey monster that had just pulled up in front of her own pathetic little excuse for a car caused a peculiar fluttering way down in her stomach.

'It isn't what you think, Jodie,' Sienna told her when her friend continued to stand there agog. 'You've got a one-track mind where anyone who isn't hitched and as happy as you are—i.e. single and content—is concerned.'

'Don't give me that!' Jodie pooh-poohed, sending her a sceptical glance. 'You're too young to settle for contentment, and you can't hang on to the past for ever.'

'Well, perhaps content's the wrong word, but I'm adjusting to my life,' she admitted, only just stopping short of telling Jodie that the last thing she wanted was another man in her life. 'So if you're thinking I'd consider making a match with Niall's brother, then I'm afraid you're going to have to think again. He's far too arrogant, overbearing and too darn cocksure of himself ever to qualify as a contender for my affections, and—' She broke off, enquiring of her friend, 'What's wrong with your mouth?

Jodie was pulling faces, Sienna decided, as Shadow would have done, if he'd been able to, the day he'd rolled on that wasp-infested chocolate wrapper. When Jodie didn't answer, however, she went on, 'He's too rich, he's got a freezer cabinet for a heart and is about as approachable as a turned on water cannon. I wouldn't sleep with Conan Ryder if he was the last man on— *What?*'

Jodie's eyes had come into the equation now. But even as it dawned on Sienna what her neighbour was trying to tell her, too late she felt that prickling awareness she always felt when Conan Ryder was close, and caught his deep voice, low in her ear, as he told her, 'Don't worry. You won't have to. We have enough rooms in Provence for the family not to have to share with the guests.'

Those cool words were at variance with the warmth of his breath against her hair—an unintentional caress that sent tingles along her very nerve-endings. Or was it so unintentional? she wondered, her pulse quickening ridiculously. Because she didn't think he'd miss a single trick to try and unsettle her.

Impelled by good manners to introduce him to Jodie, she tried to shake off the devastating effects of Conan's nearness. But before she could find her voice Jodie was shooting out a hand for him to take.

'I'm Jodie Fisher,' she pre-empted, smiling broadly at the dynamic-looking man whose bronzed chest oozed virility through a fine and fitted short-sleeved cream shirt, and whose long legs were encased in dark tailored trousers. Her cheeks were unusually flushed. Even being happily married and pregnant didn't stop a woman trying to get herself noticed by him, Sienna thought despairingly.

'The pleasure's all mine, Jodie.' His manner was charm personified. Never once in all the time she had known him had he smiled at *her* like that—with such sincere warmth—Sienna realised, annoyed with herself for even thinking it, and telling herself she hardly cared.

'Well, I'll be getting back to my hovel...' Still beaming, Jodie gestured towards the immaculately painted house next door for Conan's benefit. It made Sienna's look rather tired and dull in comparison. 'Daisy's in the garden with Shadow,' she told Sienna. 'Have a lovely time, won't you?' From the look she angled towards Conan as she was going out of the gate it was obvious what she meant.

'You'd better come in.' Alone with him, Sienna was determined not to let it bother her. 'We're nearly ready.'

Daisy was standing mixing play dough on a low table as they came out through the little galley kitchen, chattering happily to her pink hippopotamus, seated on a tiny chair, and the dog, which was stretched out with its head raised, listening interestedly to every word of the childish patter.

'You've got no qualms about leaving a four-year-old with that animal?' Conan's disapproval was obvious.

'No. Why should I have?' Sienna shot back at him over her shoulder. 'Shadow would protect her rather than cause her any harm. "That animal"—as you call him—is as gentle as a lamb!'

Peeved by his attitude, which even now questioned her suitability as a mother, she had to bite back the desire to tell him to mind his own business as she plastered on a smile and called out to Daisy, 'Come here, poppet! There's somebody I want you to meet.'

Grabbing her hippopotamus, the little girl ran up to them.

'Do you remember…Mr Ryder?' Sienna queried after some hesitation. For some reason *Uncle Conan* didn't spring easily to her lips—which was crazy, she realised, because that was who he was.

The little girl gazed coyly up at him, her hazel eyes studying him with a seriousness way beyond her years. Eventually she asked, 'Are you my daddy?' and something squeezed painfully around Sienna's heart.

Daisy had never known Niall—not properly anyway. And she certainly couldn't remember him. So wasn't it an obvious mistake for her to imagine that Conan might be her father?

Dropping to his haunches, Conan gazed—transfixed—at the little girl who was studying him so intently, and something ripped through him, taking his breath away.

It was Niall at four years old! Niall with his shock of bright hair and his sturdy little body and his frowning bewilderment at the world as he'd looked to him—his older brother—for answers…

The feeling in his chest was almost suffocating. Somehow, though, he recovered himself enough to respond to her question about being her father. 'No, Daisy, I'm not,' he murmured huskily.

Had she imagined that crack in his voice? Sienna wondered, noticing how long and tanned and utterly masculine his hands were as they clasped the tiny arms, although he stopped short of actually catching Daisy to him. But she *was* his late brother's child, and for the first time it struck Sienna just how much pain the separation between her and Niall's family might have caused them—all of them. It was something far too uncomfortable to dwell on.

'This is Daddy's brother. Your Uncle Conan. Do you remember me telling you about the little holiday we're going on today?' Daisy's shining curls caught the sunlight as she nodded zealously. 'He's come to take us back with him to see your grandmother.'

Daisy looked quickly across at the dog, which hadn't come running up to this disapproving stranger as he had the last time, but was keeping at a very safe distance today. 'And Shadow?'

'And Shadow,' Sienna echoed firmly, with a challenging lift of her chin towards Niall's brother. So he didn't like her dog? Well, too bad! Perhaps if she was lucky she could get Shadow to slobber all over him and shed hairs over the back seat of his stupendously expensive car!

'What about Hippo? Can I take him too?'

'Of course you can,' Sienna said warmly. Slicing a glance down at Conan's gleaming black hair, she wondered what he was thinking when his interest shifted from his niece to the rather worn and faded toy she was clutching.

Had he remembered *he* had bought it, for Daisy's first birthday? she wondered. And that with it he had brought a remarkably expensive bottle of champagne? A gift for her and Niall because it was their second wedding anniversary. Niall had telephoned only minutes before and apologised for not being able to get home early as promised for Daisy's birthday, without a word about their own celebration. She recalled feeling stupidly hurt, thinking how strange it was that Conan had remembered when his brother hadn't. But then Niall had had a lot on his mind, had been working hard for his little family. And he'd fallen over himself with remorse when he had come home just after midnight and seen the bottle of champagne that Conan had left. He'd made it up to her the next day with chocolates and flowers, promising never— *ever*—to forget again…

Battling with the turmoil of emotions going on inside her, she saw Conan's mouth compress in brief recognition of the gift he had given his niece. But then his hands dropped away from the little girl and, getting to his feet again, towering above them both, he said with a coldness that seemed to leave him untouched, 'Well? Are we ready to go?'

CHAPTER THREE

FROM luxury saloon to private jet, to the equally luxurious chauffeur-driven car that had been waiting for them at the airport, the journey to Provence had been as smooth and as hassle-free as only the journeys of men as mega-rich as Conan Ryder could be. A discreet cabin crew had catered for their every need while Conan worked on his laptop in a separate compartment of the plane, keeping Sienna topped up with refreshments and occupying Daisy with games and the odd edible treat. Even Shadow had slept most of the way, in the large, comfortable carrier provided for the purpose, oblivious to the fact that he was being whisked thousands of feet up over a glittering body of water, and down across vast swathes of unfenced and sunlit fields.

Now, with the concrete and the crowds of the bustling mainland coast behind them, they were travelling across wild and isolated land jutting out into a sparkling sea.

It was another world, Sienna thought, gazing at the tall pine trees that defined the landscape and concealed exclusive walled mansions from prying eyes. A world far removed from the one she knew. A billionaire's retreat.

As the car slowed to pass through electrically operated gates into the lush, meandering grounds of Conan's hideaway, Sienna gulped back a gasp. What she was looking at was no less than magnificent. A huge white modern terracotta-roofed villa built on various levels, with a profusion of flower draped balconies, balustrades and floor to ceiling windows enjoying dramatic views of the rocky coast above which they were perched, of looming mountains and a breath-catching expanse of azure water.

Conan was sitting in the front of the car, conversing with his driver in amazingly fluent French, and had said very little to her since leaving the airport.

Viewing his dark and striking profile with the same mixture of wonder and appreciation with which she would view a classical marble statue as he turned and laughed at something the chauffeur had said, she resolved never to let him see just how overwhelmed she was by his wealth and his dauntingly impressive house—or by him!

Sitting immediately behind him, however, little Daisy had no such qualms.

As the car drew to a standstill at the end of the long drive, she exclaimed excitedly, 'Is this where we're going to live?'

'Yes, Daisy.' Conan's voice was decisive, causing Sienna to look at him quickly with a little trickle of unease.

'For ever and ever?'

Ignoring her mother's questioning glare—deliberately, Sienna felt—Conan laughed rather menacingly, she thought. 'I think even you would tire of such delightful surroundings eventually.'

'No, I wouldn't,' the little girl lobbed back, certain of it. And if that conversation wasn't enough to unsettle Sienna, then her daughter's continuing enthusiasm made sure of it as Daisy asked her uncle, 'Are you going to live with us too?'

Trying to reject the unwelcome connotations inspired by that innocent enough question, as Conan's glance sliced across hers with something mocking in those green-gold eyes, she uttered quickly for his as well as her daughter's benefit, 'It's just a holiday, Daisy. Just for a few weeks. That's all.'

Something firmed the hard line of that sculpted masculine mouth, but the arrival of a couple of male members of staff to deal with their bags and let a grateful Shadow out of the back of the car precluded whatever he had been about to say.

Out of the car before Conan could come round to assist her, Sienna moved to catch Daisy's hand to stop her running on ahead. Or perhaps, subconsciously, she needed the little girl's support as much as her daughter usually needed hers, Sienna thought self-deprecatingly, nervous at suddenly finding herself on this unfamiliar, unfriendly, exclusively Ryder territory.

Surprisingly, though, Daisy made a small protest and tugged away from her, causing something not unlike resentment to rush up inside Sienna as the little girl ran over to grasp Conan's hand.

This unexpected action caught Conan totally unawares. With a sharp intake of breath that caused his chest to rise beneath the tailored shirt and his wide shoulders to stiffen, he glanced down at the little face beaming up at him, a blend of surprise and resistance coursing through his long, lean body.

'And to what do I owe this pleasure?' he asked the little girl.

Suddenly not sure of what to make of this tall, inflexible stranger, Daisy lost her courage, letting go of his hand. It still didn't deter her from skipping along beside him, or from shrugging off her mother's hand as it shot out to restrain her.

'Get used to it, Sienna,' Conan advised, quietly so that none of the others could hear. 'You've had her to yourself long enough, and now you're going to have to accept that she has other family she needs to get to know and spend time with. And if you can manage to curb your tongue with my mother while you're here you'll be doing us all a favour. As I've already explained, she's very unwell.'

Peeved by his smug and condescending attitude, itching to remind him that it was *she* who had been on the receiving end of Avril Ryder's disdain and disparaging remarks in the past, Sienna decided it wouldn't help to promote good relations between them and considered it best to remain silent.

Ignoring him, she called to Shadow, who was already sniffing his way round one of the marble pillars at the top of the steps, and was relieved when the dog bounded down to her at once.

There was solace to be found in ruffling his fur, Sienna decided, speaking soothingly to the animal as she attached a lead to his red tartan collar.

A member of staff took the dog as soon as they entered the house, and Sienna had the disconcerting feeling that she was relinquishing all her power to Conan Ryder.

'Don't worry. He'll be adequately catered for,' he assured her evenly, wise to her silent objection.

'But will he be *cared* for?' Sienna argued in protest. 'He was ill treated before he was rescued and needs special handling. He likes tea, and the odd bowl of tomato soup, and he always sleeps on my bed because he doesn't like being left in the dark.'

'Give me strength...' Those dark fringed eyes rolled skyward. 'He's a *dog,*' Conan reminded her, sounding exasperated.

So are you. She mouthed it at him with a scowl, across Daisy's bouncing curls, not wanting anyone else to witness what she knew was a very childish retaliation. But Conan Ryder was as hard and impervious to human frailty as his brother had always led her to believe he was—as she had witnessed herself in his treatment of his younger sibling. So what chance did a mere animal have against so much indifference and superiority?

A young maid called Claudette showed her and Daisy to their rooms on the first floor. Each had its own luxurious bathroom, and both bedrooms reflected more of what Sienna had seen so far of the villa's décor. Light, airy and spacious, with tasteful and predominantly white furniture, Daisy's room was smaller, and had touches of pink in its floral bedspread and at the windows. Sienna couldn't help thinking it had been chosen especially for her. The room was also just a step away from Sienna's across the wide landing.

Conan was waiting for them in the marble-floored hall when they came back downstairs a short time later, and Daisy ran to him at once, just as she had outside.

For a moment, with that determined little hand clutching his, Conan felt the same surge of resistance as he had experienced before—like a barrier slamming down on his emotions. But the little girl was giggling up at him, as though defying him to try and frighten her off again, and, yielding a little, he allowed her merely a glimmer of a smile before casting an inscrutable glance towards Sienna.

Was that triumph in his eyes? she wondered. Because while he seemed not to overly welcome his niece's attention, she felt that after what he had said outside he was putting up with it simply to needle her.

His scrutiny, though, was causing her pulses to leap-frog.

Now, tingling from the way his gaze ran over her freshly brushed hair and the golden slope of her shoulders beneath her sundress, Sienna stepped out of the beautiful house onto a sun terrace above a garden that tumbled down to the rocky shoreline and the restless sea.

Avril Ryder was propped up on a recliner in the canopied shade of the terrace, a flower-draped pergola behind her filling the air with some exotic scent. A creamy throw over her legs, she looked thinner, Sienna decided, her hair greyer than she remembered beneath a wide-brimmed floppy hat.

'Oh, there you are!' Her smile for Conan faded as her gaze shifted to Sienna, her eyes keenly assessing behind tinted lenses. Without a word to her former daughter-in-law, however, she turned her attention to Daisy, still clutching the man's hand. 'At last!' The transformation in the woman's face was like the sun coming out after a long hard winter. Her smile was warm and genuine, lending a glimmer of life to the otherwise waxen face. 'Come here, child. Let me see you.'

Daisy ran to her without hesitation and let the painfully thin arms engulf her. Too thin, Sienna decided, silently shocked at Niall's mother's appearance. No wonder Conan was worried about her, she thought, aware now that he must be far more concerned than he was letting on.

Impassively, however, she murmured, 'This is your grandmother, Daisy.'

Looking up at the pale and weary-looking face, Daisy giggled and asked, 'Why are you wearing that funny hat?'

Sienna bit the inside of her lip, expecting the pale lips to tighten as she had seen them do so often in the past. But instead they were curving in a soft smile. 'To keep the sun off my head. It doesn't look all that pretty, does it? But it does its job.'

Sienna watched Daisy digest this for a moment. 'Are you really going to be my grandmother?' she enquired. 'I've always wanted two. My friend Zoe has two. Are you going to take me to the beach like my Aunty Nanny?'

Sienna could have sworn there were tears in the shaded eyes that had suddenly turned her way.

'It's what she calls Mum,' she explained simply with a little shrug. At forty-eight, Faith Swann considered herself far too young to be called a grandmother.

'And you, Sienna…?' A bony hand was stroking the soft tumble of Daisy's curls, those tired eyes continually returning to the child's face as though they couldn't get enough of what they were seeing. A shaft of pain sliced viciously through Sienna as she wondered if her mother-in-law had noticed Daisy's likeness to her lost son. 'How have you been?'

Sienna's response was tentative. 'I'm fine.' This was hardly the same woman who had made her constantly aware that she wasn't good enough for Niall—who had ultimately blamed her for what had happened to her younger son.

'I think we should leave them for a little while, don't you?'

Sienna stiffened at the firm, masculine hand around her elbow, and caught Conan's reprimand, low and lethally soft against her ear.

'You can't possibly object?'

She couldn't tell him that her reluctance sprang from spending any more time than she had to alone with *him*.

'No,' she said tensely. 'I don't object.'

'Good.' The eyes that roamed speculatively across her face told her that the small inflexion in her voice hadn't escaped him. He gestured for her to precede him through the pergola along the pale stonework of a shrub-bordered, sun-baked path.

'I didn't realise your mother was so...unwell,' she said hesitantly, concerned. 'Unwell' seemed far too moderate a word to describe Avril Ryder's appearance. 'Is she going to be all right?'

'I sincerely hope so.' The skin was drawn tightly over Conan's hard-boned cheeks and Sienna realised he *was* far more worried than he was letting on.

'Perhaps having Daisy here will help?' she offered, feeling that same tug of remorse over having denied Niall's family the right to see his daughter.

'Yes.' The single syllable seemed dragged through Conan's clenched teeth. It was clear he was thinking along the same lines, she thought, feeling chastened. 'And you, Sienna. What have you been doing for the past three years?'

A slim shoulder lifted slightly beneath her floral print sundress—a cool blend of white and soft blues and greens, teamed that morning with a green lacy cropped bolero, which she had discarded as soon as they had stepped off the plane.

'This and that. Training for my diplomas and the rest of my gym qualifications. Visiting Mum and Dad.'

'In Spain.'

It wasn't a question, she was quick to realise. He had obviously been informed. It was just another black mark against her in the Ryder family's eyes, she'd always felt. That she was the daughter of a mere carpenter, who had sold up everything he had to go and run a wine bar for British ex-patriots with his wife on the Costa del Sol!

'And what about the man whose flat you were

sharing the night your husband died?' His tone had turned as hard as the earth they were skirting on either side of the path, where an endless profusion of white roses made her almost heady with their fragrance. 'How long did *he* stay in the picture?'

'I'd rather not discuss it, if you don't mind,' she responded, turning away.

Her profile, he noticed, was proud and challenging, yet insufferably alluring. He felt that stirring in his blood, that primal desire he had always recognised for his late brother's wife, and always violently rejected with every bone in his body.

'I bet you wouldn't!'

Sienna's expression as she looked his way again was almost careless, her pink creamy lips set in a sexy pout. He had the almost unbearable urge to crush them beneath his, to feel her body stir as his was stirring—and the evidence would be apparent if he carried on thinking like this! he thought censoriously.

She gave a little shrug, nonchalant and dismissive, as though her actions in the past were of no consequence whatsoever. That action caused the strap of her dress suddenly to slip off her shoulder. Its bareness was provocative, like pale silk begging for his touch.

Sienna reached for the fallen strap, sucking in

her breath as Conan did the same, getting to it before she could and slipping it back on her shoulder.

'Thank you,' she murmured, breathless from the shocking electrical impulses zinging through her at the merest touch of his hand.

'When did you have that done?' He meant her tattoo, and his voice was cool, composed, holding none of the turmoil that was going on inside her.

'On my eighteenth birthday.'

Something tugged at his mouth. 'Before you knew better.'

She ignored that statement, because that's what it was. Her tattoo was just another thing he didn't like about her, she realised, telling herself quite adamantly that she didn't care.

'Daisy has a lot of energy,' she expressed, wanting to get away from him and his flower-filled garden, finding both disturbing with her troubling awareness of his far too unsettling proximity. 'Do you think that leaving her with Avril for too long is a good idea?'

They had stopped on the path. 'For my mother's welfare?' From beneath his dark lashes he regarded her with a contemplative amusement. 'Or for yours, Sienna?'

Her throat going dry, she swallowed. Goodness! The man was perceptive!

'Why should I be concerned for *my* welfare?' she bluffed, her heart rate quickening, pretending not to understand as she sent a glance seawards to where a flotilla of sailboats sported their jaunty colours as they skirted the peninsula.

'Why are you always so jittery when you're alone with me?'

'I'm not jittery.' Who was she kidding? 'Why should it make me jittery being alone with you?'

'You tell me.'

The warmth of the sun on her skin was a sensuality she could well have done without, and the hum of Mediterranean insects only emphasised the pregnant silence between them.

'Is it because I'm the only one who knows your secret, Sienna?'

She looked at him quickly, her eyes hooded and wary. 'My secret?'

Her tone, Conan noted, was tinged with alarm. What else had she been hiding for those two and a half years she'd been married to his brother?

'The only one who knows the kind of girl you really are,' he elaborated.

'You *think* you know. *Knew,*' she corrected emphatically.

He laughed softly. 'Whose so-called "shopping trips" to London and all those wanderings around museums were just a smokescreen for an illicit affair.'

About to deny it strongly, she felt the significance of what he'd meant when he said he was the only one who knew suddenly dawn on her, so that unthinkingly she asked, 'You didn't tell your mother about your suspicions?' She found that amazing. 'You surprise me, Conan.' She would have thought he wouldn't miss a chance to tell Avril exactly what he believed he'd discovered.

'And break her heart more than it was broken already to find that her son's wife was cheating on him? Don't you think she was devastated enough?'

Emotionlessly, because she would never give Niall's brother the satisfaction of knowing how much she had been through herself, she uttered, 'Your discretion becomes you.'

'Which is more than could be said for your morals.'

'Yes, well…' Heated colour crept across her cheeks. 'That was what you wanted to believe. You wouldn't listen to anything I said when I tried to explain.'

'That you and this Timothy Leicester were just good friends?' He laughed again, more harshly this time. 'It's a worn-out cliché.'

'No, we were more—much more than that,

Conan.' Her gaze glanced across his, hard and defiant. She recognised from the rigidity of his jaw the danger that lay in provoking him, and yet it was a danger unlike any she had known before...

It would be sheer folly to antagonise him, or to deliberately fuel his hostility towards her, and so she burst out truthfully, 'I was never unfaithful to Niall. I loved him!' It was wrung from the anguished depths of her heart.

'You'll forgive me if I don't wholly acknowledge the authenticity of that statement. After all, we both know your capacity for telling lies.' They were walking again, and with a courtesy that was incongruous with the harshness of his words he stopped to lift a low branch of oleander that was growing over the path, its stems heavy with pink blossoms, their sultry scent impinging on the air.

Sienna moved under it and felt her hair lightly brush his arm. The contact was unwelcome, unwanted and electrifying.

'Which brings me to the other reason.'

'Other reason?' She dragged her gaze from the blue water of a pool she had spotted on another level of the garden, glancing warily up at him as he let the branch go and fell into step beside her. 'For what?'

'For why you've always made every excuse under the sun to limit the time you spend alone with me.'

Had she? She hadn't been conscious of it.

Heart beating erratically, she responded, 'Simple. I just don't like your company.'

'That goes without saying. But it isn't just my company that disturbs you, is it, Sienna?'

What was it then? she wondered, glancing out at the last of the sailboats that were still within her vision on the sparkling water. Because she wasn't sure. Even when she'd been married to his brother Conan had disturbed her beyond belief. It was that raw animal energy that positively crackled from him that she found so unsettling, even without the dark enigma of his character, or the penetrating green-gold of eyes that seemed to strip her of her every secret—along with her floundering self-confidence—on those few occasions that she had come in contact with him. Eyes that assessed, judged and unhinged her so much that she was always glad to escape.

His ability to unsettle her, she realised despairingly, had only intensified with the years. But now, striving for equanimity, she murmured, 'I really don't know what you're talking about.'

'Don't you?' His smile was feral. 'Oh, I think you do.'

She wasn't sure when they had stopped walking, but now she felt the snare of those glacial green-gold eyes holding her as though in an invisible trap.

'I'm talking about sex, Sienna.'

With her heart suddenly hammering against her ribcage, she echoed, 'Sex?' She uttered a brittle little laugh. 'With you?' Her mouth contorted at the concept of such an idea, masking the furore of wild sensations going on inside her.

Conan's lips moved wryly, mocking, unperturbed. 'Well, I wouldn't have put it quite so graphically as that,' he stated, watching the colour rise in her cheeks and seeming to relish every ounce of her discomfiture. 'I was talking chemistry—unlikely though I know that seems. But then since when did physical attraction ever have anything to do with *liking* the object of one's attraction, or even respecting them for that matter? And I know your respect for me is about as low on the scale of one to a thousand as mine is for you.'

'That makes it all right, then, doesn't it?' she snapped. 'I often get my kicks out of shacking up with men I can't stand the sight of!'

'Or with those who keep you in enough luxury to buy your affection until you find more interesting diversions elsewhere.'

'Like I did with Niall, I suppose?' she jibed.

'You might think it's something to hold up as a trophy, Sienna, but I don't. My brother was besotted with you.'

'Yes,' she acknowledged, closing her eyes, clenching her teeth against the well of emotion that threatened to engulf her, the unshed tears that were locked inside her and seemed doomed never to know the mercy of release.

Niall *had* been besotted. Adoring. Almost obsessive in his love for her, so that sometimes she'd felt stifled by the possessiveness that had sprung from his insecurities. She'd been someone to flaunt. To show off. To place on a pedestal so high that sometimes she'd been frightened of toppling off. And sometimes she'd felt—to use Conan's own words—like a trophy, a feather in Niall's cap to parade over the man he'd most wanted to impress: his richer, harder-headed and far more successful older brother.

As he watched the emotions that chased across her face, a groove deepened between Conan's thick eyebrows. Was she telling him the truth? Had she ever really loved his brother? Was that what was tormenting her? Plain and simple guilt? Or was it something else altogether?

'Remorse, Sienna?' He reached out and slid a hand around the nape of her neck. He heard her breath catch, felt her body stiffen, the pulse beneath his fingers beating a frenzied rhythm.

'What are you hoping?' To her own ears she sounded afraid, and her breathlessness was betraying to him that it was herself she was afraid of, the sensations that were ripping through her just from the touch of those cool fingers on her heated skin. 'That I'll fall for you so you can dump me? Because that's about as likely as one of our spacecraft finding life on Mars tomorrow night!'

Way off in the distance the buzz of a speedboat encroached on the peaceful garden. Closer to hand, a gentle breeze played among the spiky leaves of the oleander tree.

'I've always lived by the premise that's anything's likely.' A complacent smile touched his lips. 'And we both know you weren't impervious to me even with two other lovers in the picture—don't we, Sienna?'

Fear clouded her eyes. 'You read it all wrong!'

'Did I?'

He was referring to the firm's dinner-dance that she had attended with Niall. Niall had been drinking with clients at the bar, trying to tie down a deal. Conan had come over to the table where she had been sitting alone and asked her to dance—just out of courtesy, she'd guessed.

In a dark evening suit, white winged collar shirt and bow tie, he'd looked particularly spectacular—hard and confident and sophisticated—and he'd had the air about him of a man you couldn't say no to—as he always had in his private life as well as in business.

She remembered the feel of that impeccably clad arm going around her as they'd taken to the floor. The way every nerve in her body had seemed to tense like a tuned up violin as his hand burned through the flimsy red fabric of her dress.

'The telltale flush on those beautiful cheeks…' Conan's words as he remembered shook Sienna back to the present. They seemed to have given him licence to trace the fine structure of her face. His fingers were long and skilful and she couldn't seem to stop him, held in thrall by a sensuality that was as dangerous as it was thrilling as he continued reminiscing. 'The dilated pupils. That nervous stammer that sprang from between those alluring and very provocative lips.'

I felt awkward with you! Embarrassed! But there was a reason for it! There was a reason for everything I did!

But she couldn't tell him that.

Don't tell anyone! For a fleeting moment the words echoed through her brain—anguished and imploring. *Promise me you'll never tell anyone! Especially Conan!*

She felt straitjacketed by her emotions—just as she had then. But she had made a promise and she would never renege on that promise, she thought bitterly. Not now. Not ever.

Facing the censuring clarity of that glittering gold gaze, she said with a forced air of resignation, 'Well, there you have me! It seems you were irresistible, doesn't it, Conan? But not any more.'

He laughed softly as he lifted her chin with a curved forefinger, noting the way her breath shivered through her nostrils before his gaze rested on the trembling lashes that half veiled the darkening blue of her eyes. 'No?' he murmured silkily.

'Aren't you worried I might try to *bleed you dry?*' she emphasised, taunting him with it, pulling back from him on legs that felt so much like jelly she was wondering how much longer they could hold her.

He merely laughed again, and said, 'You couldn't bleed me dry.'

Of course. He had far too many millions for that.

A deep bark followed by a childlike squeal of laughter filtered down from the terrace above them. To Sienna it was a welcome reprieve.

'Go and make yourself at home. Settle in,' Conan

advised with a jerk of his chin towards where the sounds were coming from. 'But remember…you're playing a dangerous game, Sienna. You won't find me half so much of a push-over as my brother.'

She almost ran from him, back along the path, eager only for the safe, simple demands of Daisy and Shadow.

CHAPTER FOUR

CONAN looked up from the laptop and out of his study window, relinquishing his interest in the spreadsheet he was updating in favour of the more interesting scene by the pool.

In a skimpy white crop-top and shorts, Sienna was engaged in a workout. Daisy was crayoning in a sketchbook on the marble tiles in the shade of the sun-umbrella above the table just behind her. The hairy mutt, he noted with a derogatory grimace, was lounging nearby.

His niece was stocky, like her father, he decided, some uninvited emotion softening the firm line of his mouth. She wouldn't ever inherit her mother's petite figure, but she was a well-behaved and pleasant child, he'd observed since their arrival two days ago, and if she lacked any sort of maternal control then it certainly wasn't evident.

Which was one point in her mother's favour if nothing else, he acknowledged rather reluctantly, surprised by the way just the thought of another sparring session with his brother's unscrupulous little widow could kick his libido into life, sending a burning ache down through the centre of his hardening anatomy.

Or was it just the way she was moving with those weights strapped to her ankles? Her slim, beautifully shaped legs lifting independently, her small breasts accentuated, as she lay with her hands behind her head, face turned upwards to the sun?

At that moment the little girl ran up to her. He watched Sienna sit up, saw her smile as she pushed the hair out of the child's eyes. The tender action reminded him of those times on the periphery of his memory with his own mother, when there had been just the two of them—before everything had changed after Avril had married his stepfather and then given birth to Niall. He had learned to harden himself against moments like these—against those early memories—and he did it now, saving the data on his laptop and closing down the program he had been using.

Whether he was happy about it or not, he thought, Sienna was his guest, and relations between her and his mother had been strained to say the least since he had brought her back with him. That was probably why she had chosen to come out to the pool area now, while Avril was up in her room taking a nap. She had definitely been going out of her way to avoid too much contact with his mother, with the result that she was spending far too much time alone. Something he intended to rectify as of now!

Standing with legs apart, ankle-weights substituted with hand- weights, her body angled, with her raised arm forming a perfect arc above her head, Sienna lost track of the seconds she'd been maintaining the position as Conan appeared, coming across the terrace in a white linen shirt and pale chinos.

His masculinity was glaringly evident in the corded strength of his throat above the open 'V' of his collar and in the larger 'V' of dark body hair shading his chest beneath his shirt. His chinos were fitted enough to reveal the narrow-hipped strength of his lower body, and the taut musculature of his thighs. His feet were thrust into backless leather mules, as fit and tanned and virile as the rest of him.

Spotting him, Daisy scrambled to her feet, already running up to him with her colouring book.

His reluctant smile for the little girl made Sienna's stomach twinge with something indefinable before he squatted down on his haunches to look at the picture his niece was showing him. She caught his soft words of praise—not gushing, but understatedly genuine—before he said something else more quietly that had the little girl darting off in the direction of the house.

'Take the dog with you, Daisy,' his deep voice instructed, and an obedient click of her tongue had Shadow leaping up and bounding after her.

Sienna straightened from the exercise she'd been doing with her hand-weights, letting both her arms hang at her sides. Her heart rate was usually up a bit after she'd finished a workout, she realised, but the sight of Conan had her blood pounding as though she'd been running hard.

'Does everyone do what you tell them to?'

His smile was wry. 'Usually.'

She didn't doubt it—especially those who were on his substantial payroll. He was the type of man for whom waiters and porters materialised like genies, while others, like Daisy and Shadow, vanished at will.

'I thought you were working? Avril said you were working at home today.'

Did he think she was gabbling? She certainly sounded as though she was.

'I was,' he said, coming closer. And when she could only stand and look at him, rooted to the spot by the breath-catching spell of his very aura, he added, 'I saw you from my study. I decided the time had come not to have you spending so much time on your own.'

She smiled a rather nervous smile. 'Did you bribe Daisy with some particular treat to get her out of the way?'

He made another wry movement with his mouth. 'Now, what on earth makes you think that?'

'I think you could bribe your way out of anything you wanted to.'

He laughed—a warm, deep sound that had her reminding herself of how ruthless he was when she realised she was in danger of forgetting it. 'I simply told her that Claudette has taken some pastries up to my mother, and that Avril has asked Daisy to join her.'

'That's nice,' Sienna expressed, glad at least that her daughter was forming a bond with her new grandmother, even if *she* wasn't.

Those slow strides brought him nearer, and Sienna's breath caught almost audibly in her lungs.

'May I?'

She handed him the moderate weights she was still clutching in her tense fingers, watching him assess their poundage, weighing them both together in one tanned and strikingly tapered hand.

Crazily, for a moment she considered those hands making a calculated assessment of her body, feeling, touching, moulding…

Shocked by the disturbing imagery, mentally she shook it away. 'I'm not hoping to be Mr Universe,' she elucidated, a little more sharply than she had intended when she saw his mouth twist almost mockingly. 'Just to keep myself toned up.' Perhaps he considered those weights light, but then in those strong brown hands four times as much probably would be! she thought, shaken by her wayward thoughts about him.

'I should hope not.' She could feel his gaze travelling down over her figure where a moment ago she had imagined his hands travelling the same path. 'You're perfectly acceptable as you are.'

Wishing she'd worn a bra, with a rush of colour to her cheeks she felt the betraying thrust of her breasts against the stretchy fabric of her top.

'The last time I saw you at a poolside you were wearing a swimsuit from Dior,' he reminded her, concluding his disconcerting survey of her body. 'And you were positively dripping with gold.'

Gold she had sold—along with all her other jewellery, her fast car, and the rest of the things he obviously believed she'd cared about! she thought bitterly. To pay off the debts she'd been left with after Niall had died.

'That wasn't me!'

'Wasn't it?' He laughed again, not so warmly this time, the sinews working in his strong throat. 'I'd recognise that figure anywhere—although I'd agree that nowadays you're certainly...fully toned.'

His scrutiny of her was electrifying, moving as it did with slow deliberation over the golden slopes of her shoulders, touching on the firm, yet willowy arms, and coming to rest with appreciative male satisfaction on the betraying fullness of her breasts.

'I mean it wasn't...' How could she explain to him how ostentatious she'd found that jewellery? How she'd worn it merely to please Niall, because he had bought it for her? And that the extortionately pricey swimsuit hadn't been something she would even have dreamt of buying for herself— let alone considered wearing! That she'd only been persuaded to after Niall had presented her with it as a substitute for the plainer, less tantalising one she'd chosen herself from her favourite high street store? 'I was a different person then, Conan,' she said tonelessly, with a dryness creeping up her throat. 'We all were.'

His sensuous mouth moved in contemplation

before he laid the weights down with that casual grace of his on one of the glass poolside tables.

'Were we?' he remarked, turning his full attention back to her again. 'Does a leopard ever change its spots?'

'No, apparently not!' she flung back at him, hurting and angry, because there was no way that he would ever change his opinion of her. His prejudices were set in stone! 'I'm not staying here talking to you when you only came out here to try and antagonise me!'

She made to move past him, but the table was blocking her way on one side, and as she moved to go around the other he side-stepped, so that she couldn't pass without the risk of falling into the pool.

His hands were raised palm-outwards in defence against her verbal attack. 'Believe me—that wasn't my intention.'

'Wasn't it?' Hot colour stained her cheeks. Her eyes, in contrast, were dark and accusing. 'You wouldn't miss a trick in trying to have a go at me. You might think I'm guilty of sleeping around during my marriage, but at least I wasn't the one lusting after my brother's wife!'

Her words seemed to stun him rigid.

Feeling the waves of condemnation burning

from him, and already regretting her rash remark, Sienna darted a glance around for the quickest means of escape.

'Would you mind repeating that statement?' he rasped, in a dangerously low voice.

Yes, I would! she thought hectically, wishing she could retract it. And, shamed into flight—desperate to get away from him—she turned and plunged headlong into the pool.

She had only swum a few metres when she heard the deep splash behind her, felt herself being rocked by the displacement of water, and realised with a small gasp of alarmed amazement that Conan was giving chase—fully clothed!

She did a blazing front-crawl to the other side of the pool, reaching it with a determined grab for the tiled edge. But with a small gasp of dismay she heard Conan coming up behind her, felt a strong, determined hand pulling her round.

For endless pulsing moments they glared angrily at each other, the sun beating down a relentless observer, striking bronze from the transparency of Conan's shirt where it now clung to his skin, burning across Sienna, though not as much as she was burning inside.

She had never seen him look so wild or so untameable, and she didn't know what galvanised her into what happened next. But as his curiously ravaged face dipped low she was lifting hers to meet it, their angry passion given rein in a mutually antagonised kiss.

Conan didn't know what he had been intending to do when he'd come after her, but this, he realised, plundering her soft eager mouth, was the only ultimate outcome. Maybe her words had struck a raw chord in him because of his long denial of his body's uncontrolled response to her. The wanting he had never allowed himself to entertain even when he had been shocked into realising how nervous she was in his arms during that dance that night, and how he obviously affected her. Even if she refused to acknowledge it, he thought grimly. But there was no need for denial or for any reservations now.

As he shifted his arm to pull her into the rock-hard length of his body Sienna made a guttural sound deep in her throat, clawing at the warm wetness of his rippling back with desperate and greedy hands.

She hated the man, and yet…

Driven by desire, and the intensity of a passion such as she had never known before, she gave in to its demands, letting her trembling hands slide up to tangle in the soaked black thickness of his hair, responding to that hungry, insistent masculine mouth with unrelenting demands of her own.

Oh! Dear heaven... She gave a tortured groan—a low, anguished sound from deep inside her. She wanted more than this! She wanted all the things she had been imagining with him, which were responsible for the self-degradation that had had her flinging that insult at him just now. She wanted him to—

Her thoughts were driven from her mind as his hands suddenly spanned her waist, lifting her up so her legs automatically moved around him.

Supporting her with his arm, he was tilting her head back, his mouth closing over her clinging top through which her nipples were protruding in unashamed arousal. Never had she known such wanting as his actions sent red-hot spears of desire piercing down through her body, igniting a flame at the very heart of her femininity.

She could feel his own arousal, pulsing and hard, and moved against him like a wild thing as he pulled up her top so that his hands could claim the aching fullness of her eager breasts.

Sensations coursed through her, piling one on top of the other, feeding on each other. Sensations fuelled by a desire that had been driven by anger and yet which was now exploding in a furore of feelings such as she had never known.

She had been in love with his brother; she had thought she knew everything about sexual desire. But nothing in her life or in her short-lived marriage had compared with or prepared her for the driving urgency of this pure raw lust...

Cruelly she was reminded of their earlier confrontation, and of how much Conan despised her. It made her realise that was all that this...this madness was. Lust, she thought bitterly, and she wrenched herself away from him, her feet touching bottom, her face screwed up in disgust as she pulled at her top, turning her head away, unable to face the mocking derision she knew she would see in his eyes.

'What's the matter, Sienna? Can't you look at me?' His voice was surprisingly hoarse, and he sounded as breathless as she was.

Chancing a glance at him, she noticed that his eyes were fathomlessly dark, his eyelids heavy from the heat of his desire. His mouth wasn't derisive at all. The full lower lip pulled was taut, as if he was having some inner battle for control. Beneath that tantalisingly transparent shirt she could see the way his chest was rising and falling heavily.

'I didn't intend that to happen either,' he admitted.

'Didn't you?' Remaining hostile, she decided, was the only way of saving face. How else could she explain those moments of insanity that had gripped her? That had dictated her actions? 'I would have thought your greatest wish was to see me humiliated.'

His eyes narrowed as he searched her small, indignant features. Her eyes looked like smoky sapphires, and her mouth was pink and swollen from the mutually fierce hunger that even with all his sexual experience had still left him reeling, and so hard with wanting he felt a weakness spreading along his thighs. 'Is that how you feel?'

'What do you think?' she murmured indignantly.

'I think we were both in a state of high tension and both had to let off steam,' he stated pragmatically—almost laughably so in the circumstances.

Letting off steam! Was that all he thought it was?

Well, of course. What did you want it to be? a little voice inside Sienna jeered. He was Niall's brother—Daisy's uncle. Nothing more.

'Now, if you'll excuse me…' That familiar mockery was back on Conan's lips, yet it was incongruous with the huskiness of his voice and the inscrutable expression in his eyes. 'Much as I'd like to stay and bring this pleasurable little interlude to its natural conclusion, I have to get back to work.'

And that was going to test his powers of self-discipline more than seemed humanly possible, he realised. Although the alternative was to stay and have her believe what she had accused him of earlier. When he'd always rejected *any* conscious attraction towards his brother's wife. 'Besides… I've never made love to a woman in anger—' such behaviour was unpardonable and beneath him, he thought, fighting the long-buried demons that were threatening to surface '—and I don't intend to start now.'

With one thrust of those muscular arms he propelled himself effortlessly out of the pool, water cascading from his magnificent body.

As he walked away, Sienna broodingly noticed how his shirt clung wetly to his broad back, accentuating every muscle, and how his chinos had moulded themselves to his firm, hard buttocks and his powerful thighs. A sharp ache of unsated desire pierced her small, excruciatingly aroused body.

What had possessed her? And what must he think of her? she demanded of herself shamefully, watching discreetly from under her lashes as he scooped up the mules he'd obviously kicked off to give chase to her. Her behaviour must only have cemented his opinion of the type of girl he thought she was, she decided hopelessly, for all his remarks about them both needing to 'let off steam.'

He was a man very much in command of himself—and of his actions, she accepted reluctantly, grudgingly admiring the economy and grace with which he moved for a man of his height and build as he grabbed a towel from one of the sun loungers he was passing and began rubbing it casually over his hair. And a man who would consider the consequences of everything he did and said, she realised, even while she was resenting him. A man of surprising strength of character. Of principle, even. A man completely and utterly in control. And recognising that—along with what he had said just now about not making love in anger—caused a ridiculous ache in her throat.

'How have you been today?' Sienna asked, striving to be friendly as she came across her mother-in-law the following evening, on her usual shady seat on the terrace. 'How are you feeling?' She sank down onto the elegantly wrought, deeply cushioned chair beside her. Daisy was already in bed and Conan had been out for most of the day. She should have been relieved, she realised, and yet his absence was too noticeable to be pleasant.

'As good as I'm ever going to feel, I imagine,' Avril responded. 'The doctors can't seem to make up their minds as to what's wrong with me.' Even her rather resigned little shrug seemed like an effort. 'Can you credit that? Conan pays them a fortune and they can't even come up with a simple diagnosis. One says it's simply post-viral syndrome. Another one even stuck his neck out and suggested I have ME.'

'And you can't get about?' Sienna queried, sympathising. 'Or take any form of gentle exercise?' From casual comments Conan had made, Sienna knew he wanted his mother to try and get about more.

'Exercise?'

From the way she said it, Sienna thought, anyone would think she'd suggested a trip to the moon.

'That's the answer to everything nowadays, isn't it?' Avril remarked rather derisively. 'Especially with you younger generation.'

It was a conscious slight, Sienna decided, against all her years of training, and for a moment she felt as though she'd travelled back in time and was again the tentative, insecure creature she'd been, who'd often had to bite her tongue and had been made to feel like an interloper in her husband's family. Now, undeterred, and with a wealth of experience of working with both the fit and healthy and the elderly, she said, 'It's the answer to a lot of things.'

'Not in this case, Sienna—though your concern for me, I must say, is rather surprising.'

Because old hostilities were still there, she realised. And barely concealed where Avril was concerned.

'I don't like seeing anyone sick or suffering,' Sienna explained, brushing a rose petal from the loose white skirt she had teamed with a pale blue camisole. 'Especially when they can be repaired.'

The woman uttered a feeble laugh. 'I'm past repairing.'

'No, you're not,' Sienna returned decisively.

She was well aware that Conan's mother was little more than sixty-five, and couldn't help wondering if the woman's depression and mysterious debilitating illness had swayed her towards such fatalism. She also couldn't help thinking either how alike Niall and her mother-in-law were—in that way at least. Because her younger son had shown the same kind of resignation about a lot of things. Unlike Conan, Sienna realised intuitively, who would bend the world to his will if he had to. But then he was only Niall's half-brother, and had been born with a different set of genes…

'You know, you're much more confident than you were, Sienna.' She could feel his mother studying her from behind her smoky grey lenses. 'Confident. And much more…mature.'

'I've had to be,' Sienna remarked, cringing as she recalled the optimistic young bride Niall had first brought with him into this family circle—a circle she'd fitted into as badly as the proverbial square peg!

'You didn't have to do it alone.' She meant bringing up Daisy, and Sienna felt her stomach muscles tightening. 'Conan tells me your parents are still in Spain. And yet they get to see her?' she expressed, when Sienna nodded.

When *she* hadn't. That was clearly what the other woman was saying.

'I'm sorry.' Sienna stared at the bright blossoms draping the flower-decked pergola, not knowing, in the circumstances, how she could have done things any other way. 'I really am.'

'There were faults on both sides,' her mother-in-law was admitting surprisingly. 'I realise that now. You were far too determined. Too strong-willed for a man like Niall. And far too young to take on the responsibilities of a wife and mother. You weren't…' Her voice tailed off, as though she'd thought better of expressing her views aloud.

'I wasn't the sort of wife you would have chosen for him?' Sienna supplied crisply, remembering this family's rejection of her a little less painfully than she once had.

'I know I might have made you feel like that.' A sigh seemed to shiver through the woman's thin frame, but all she added—as though it excused everything—was, 'He was my *son*.'

Despite everything, Sienna's heart went out to her, her lungs locking tight with emotion.

She didn't want to be discussing this—raking up the past. Her memories of that time, and of the situations she had been put into, which had helped condemn her in this family's eyes, still made her smart with the injustice of it all. And there had been none more condemning or unjust than Conan's scorching censure. But then what would *anyone* have thought of a mother who'd left her sick baby to go out partying? Without even bothering to ring up and check?

No, it was worse than that. Who had deliberately switched off her phone!

She could still see the condemnation in those green-gold eyes as he'd marched her away from that party. Still remember her desperation and panic over what might be wrong with Daisy, her futile attempts to make Niall's brother believe that her little girl had been fine when she'd left the house. To try and explain.

He hadn't listened, of course. Who would have? There had been far too much evidence against her.

Sick with self-remorse, she hadn't even been able to convince herself that she hadn't been that negligent. Not until later. Not until after her name had been reduced to mud in the Ryder family's eyes and they had notched up yet another black mark against her...

'If you'd been Conan's wife he would never have indulged you in the same way my younger son seemed to want to. He might be a very wealthy man, but he's not weak-willed and easily swayed like his brother was. I'm afraid if it had been Conan you'd chosen he'd soon have pulled you into line.'

No, he wouldn't! Sienna fumed silently. Because there had been no 'pulling into line' that had needed to be done. She was surprised though to hear Avril describe her younger son as weak. 'Then I must thank my lucky stars that that's one union you're never going to see,' she said with a forced little laugh.

'Am I missing something?' Conan's deep warm voice caused goose bumps to break out over Sienna's skin.

She hadn't seen him since he'd left to attend

some business meeting that morning. Now, as
he crossed the terrace to where they were sitting,
wearing an impeccably cut silver grey suit, white
shirt and silver tie, he looked so vital and dynamic
against the backdrop of his luxury residence that
the very sight of him took Sienna's breath away.

'What have you two been talking about?' he enquired smoothly.

Her nostrils dilated at the elusive spice of his
aftershave lotion as he moved into their sphere,
her senses filling with him, her body tingling as
his gaze ran over her camisole and her feminine
skirt. In spite of her fluttering pulse, and motivated by her memories of his insensitivity and by
this frighteningly lethal power he seemed to have
over her, she looked up into those rugged features
to say pointedly, 'You.'

He was aware of the contention in her voice. It
was evident in the way his mouth twisted in mocking amusement.

'For heaven's sake, Conan, take her away and do
something with her!' Avril suggested, with more
strength than she'd seemed capable of. 'Or she'll
be having me jogging round the cape and back before I know where I am.'

'Well, that wouldn't be a bad thing, would it?'
he expressed surprisingly with a wry smile at his

mother—a smile that changed to one of heart-stopping sensuality as it came to rest on Sienna. 'It seems my mother's given me licence to do whatever I want with you...' The innuendo was unmistakable, and the light that flickered in the Celtic gold of his eyes as he offered her his hand burned with sensual mockery. 'So we'd better not disappoint her, had we?'

CHAPTER FIVE

IMPELLED by something stronger than her own will, she took the hand he was holding out to her. It was warm and strong and incredibly stimulating, sending a sharp *frisson* through her racing blood.

'Where are we going?' she asked, her fingers still in his as he brought her out across the front portico with its marble columns to the bright red convertible Ferrari standing on the drive.

'You'll see.'

'What about Daisy?' she asked, concerned, as he opened the passenger door for her.

'Daisy's asleep,' he assured her, surprising her with the knowledge that he must have checked up on his niece before joining her and Avril on the terrace. 'She's all right, I promise you.'

It came as quite a shock to realise that he was the only person whom she would have accepted that from without needing to check it out for herself. But why? she wondered, puzzled. When she didn't even like him? When he was the last man she would choose to be with? If she'd had a choice!

'I have to pick up some documents in Cannes,' he enlightened her as the Ferrari growled away. 'We won't be gone long, but I thought you might appreciate getting away from the house for an hour or so.'

Had he really thought that? she wondered, with an insidious warmth stealing through her—until she became aware of just how she was behaving.

Careful, she warned herself, realising that she was in grave danger of weakening towards him. As most women would, she accepted without any reservation, drawn as they were to those darkly aloof features and that uncompromising air of command mixed with that smoky sexuality of his that put every other man in the shade. But then they didn't know how unpitying he was, did they? she decided bitterly.

The air was pure and sweet as they drove through the forested hills, passing swathes of olive and citrus groves, and villages perched high above the sun-streaked sea.

'Do you come here very often?' she enquired, needing to say something because he wasn't.

'As often as I can. Long weekends. Bank holidays. But almost always for the summer.'

Breathing in the aromatic scents of wild herbs and lavender, Sienna returned, 'I can see why.' With its craggy coast, its mountains, and its interminable cypress trees piercing the dramatic blue of the sky, this landscape fitted him as if he was part of it. Unyielding. Implacable. Untamed. 'My parents always liked Spain, so we went there virtually every year,' she told him. 'Self-catering—that sort of thing. Cheap and cheerful, as Mum called it, but we had some great family holidays together.'

'That sounds good,' he remarked distractedly, making her wonder if he was just saying that. After all, what was camping on the Costa Brava compared with a billionaire's security-guarded villa in the South of France?

'What about you?' she murmured a little hesitantly, eager to know more about her late husband's brother. After all, he hadn't always been rich.

She knew he'd left home while still remarkably young, and according to Niall had had a variety of mundane and often laborious jobs until some lucky break and the right contacts had tested his entrepreneurial skills and set him on the road to where he was today. He'd made his fortune in telecommunications, she remembered, although his enterprises these days ranged from anything from technology to high finance. As a man, however, he was an enigma—he always had been—and he and Niall had been as different as wind and fire.

'What *about* me?' He was changing into a lower gear to take a winding road up the steep hillside, the action drawing Sienna's attention to his lean dark hand.

'Did you have family holidays?' she enquired, slamming down the lid on her speculation over how those strong skilled hands would know their way around a woman's body.

'Well, not quite as adventurous as yours sound,' he admitted dryly.

'Niall said you never knew your own father?' she ventured, aware that he'd been born illegitimate and that he might not want to talk about it.

'No,' he said uncommunicatively, seeming, from his curious glance in her direction, to have picked up on that rather breathy note in her voice at the turn her thoughts had taken about him.

'What about your stepfather?' She knew he had adopted Conan as his own son when Conan was four or five, and that the man had also given him his name.

'What about him?' His tone was frosty to say the least.

'Did you get on with him?'

'No.'

It was obvious from the lack of any further information that he clearly didn't like this probing into what was, after all, his very private life. And if she knew anything about Conan Ryder it was that he guarded his privacy like Fort Knox. His involvements with women, if reported upon, were done so with absolute discretion—such was the respect he seemed to generate with the world's media. And if he gave interviews—as he sometimes did—it was only ever in connection with the commercial side of his life. That was unless the paparazzi got hold of something they thought would be worth reporting and managed to photograph him unofficially—as they had at that airport with Petra Flax.

A covert glance at him through her dark lenses revealed a profile as harsh and forbidding as the cliffs above which they were driving, and the knuckles of those long tanned hands appeared white as they gripped the wheel.

With a little mental shrug Sienna delved into her skirt pocket for the cell phone she'd brought with her. 'Just checking on Daisy.' She felt the need to explain when he sent her an enquiring look, and guessed from the quizzical arching of his eyebrow what he was probably thinking. She hadn't always appeared to care so much.

It came back to her now—sharper than ever—

the night Niall had telephoned, insisting she meet him at that party. A party she'd had no inclination to attend. She'd gone along for the sake of his job, leaving Daisy with their babysitter, after Niall had requested her support with some clients he was trying to close a deal with.

When Conan, with a face like a marauding Norse god, had turned up at that party a few hours later, Niall had been nowhere to be seen. Later she was to discover that he'd slipped away with his clients to a casino, leaving her to bear the brunt of Conan's pulsing anger alone.

What the hell did she think she was doing? he'd demanded. Enjoying herself regardless while her child had been taken ill and his mother and the babysitter were going half out of their wits?

She'd responded to his unrepeatable accusations as to the sort of mother he thought she was with defensive anger. Hadn't she checked her mobile at least a dozen times that evening to make sure she hadn't missed any urgent messages? No one had been more paranoid than she about leaving Daisy, and everything had been fine when she had left.

But when she'd taken her phone out of her clutch bag she'd been shocked to find it was switched off, and Conan's low opinion of her had only increased tenfold.

Later, when they were alone, Niall had admitted to her that it was he who had switched off her phone. "I just wanted you to relax," she remembered him saying, feeling a bittersweet ache for how much she had loved him—trusted him then. "You're always so wound up and worrying about her unnecessarily. And I knew I had my phone on me." He just hadn't thought when he'd left the party with those clients.

He'd bought her a pendant the next day. A golden heart on a chain with a diamond piercing its centre, virtually getting down on his knees and begging her to forgive him for showing her up in such a bad light with Conan and his mother. He'd only been thinking of her after all, she'd accepted, when all the fuss had died down. And Daisy had been all right. So she'd forgiven him. As she always had, she thought poignantly. Until that last time…

Conan's stop in Cannes was a ten-minute affair while he picked up some business papers from one of the prestigious hotels there. While he was gone, Sienna marvelled at the number of equally prestigious cars, the chic shops and the chic people who were patronising them. But the crowds along the palm-fringed promenade made her appreciate why Conan had chosen to buy a house in the peace and isolation of the peninsula, and she told him so when they were on the road again.

'I'm glad you approve,' was all he said, although she couldn't help wondering if he sounded pleased.

Because it became clear as they were driving back that he really had brought her out for no other reason than to enjoy herself, she asked, 'Why are you doing this if you despise me so much?'

Behind the dark designer lenses, his eyes didn't leave the road. 'Does there have to be a reason?'

'With you?' She stole a discreet glance at his ruggedly sculpted profile and those broad shoulders—he'd removed his jacket—and her stomach did a little flip. 'Oh yes, I think so.'

'Perhaps that incident between us in the pool the other day aroused my curiosity.'

'About what?' she croaked, thinking that that wasn't all it had aroused.

'About why a couple who—to put it a little less dramatically than you put it—don't appear to like each other should find themselves in the sort of unlikely situation we found ourselves in yesterday. Because do you know what I'd really like to do with you, Sienna?'

She had a good idea, but she didn't want to acknowledge it. Her heart was hammering and her mouth felt as dry as the Sahara. 'Put me on the first plane home?' she hedged.

'That would be the most sensible course of action to take, I agree,' he admitted. 'For both our sakes.'

'Then why don't you?'

'Because there's more than just ourselves in this to consider.'

'And if there weren't?'

'Then I'd take you home to bed and not let you out of it until we'd burned this whole crazy thing out of our systems. And do you know what's making it so hard to stop myself from doing that?'

With her pulses fluttering in response to what he had just said, she quipped unsteadily, 'No doubt you're going to tell me.'

'Knowing that you want it too.'

'Now, wait a minute…!' Confusion and embarrassment reddened her cheeks beneath the healthy lustre of her windblown hair. 'Just because we shared one kiss it doesn't mean—'

'That wasn't just a kiss.'

No, it wasn't, she thought. It was a culmination of something fuelled by hostility and resentment and which had been building with unstoppable force from the moment they had set eyes on each other again.

But, taking her silence for denial, suddenly he was pulling into a lay-by.

'What are you doing?' she challenged, her heart leaping, her throat contracting painfully as he turned off the ignition.

'What do you think I'm doing?' he murmured suggestively.

She shot him a warning glance and he laughed very softly.

'I thought you might appreciate the view,' he surprised her by saying, removing his sunglasses.

They were parked on a hilltop, with the shimmering sea below them, and it felt as though there were only the two of them in the world. It was late enough for the cicadas and lizards to have begun their evening chorus, and a late finch was chirruping in the scrubland beside the car. Affected by the sounds and scents of nature, and all the beauty around them, she found the stillness of the evening brought a painful lump to her throat.

'Why did you treat Niall so badly?' It slipped out before she could stop it, subdued yet quietly direct.

'Why did *you*?' he retorted.

She didn't answer, looking away from those harshly probing eyes towards the west, where the sun was turning the sky from brilliant gold to fiery red. What would it matter what she told him now?

His brother was dead, and there were some things that couldn't be changed no matter what was said.

'Do I take it from your silence that you're admitting to that affair at last?'

Her head pivoted to face him. 'No!'

That cynical curl to his mouth told her he didn't believe her. 'Did you realise Niall was aware of it, Sienna?'

Watching the shadows that flitted across her face, Conan couldn't help thinking that she seemed shaken by his disclosure. In fact she looked positively shattered by it, he thought, surprised. But then what wife who had just found out that her husband had known about her extra-marital relationship wouldn't? he thought scornfully.

'He couldn't have been. I mean…there was nothing to be aware of,' Sienna uttered, bemused. And, as it dawned on her just what Conan was saying, 'You mean…he was the one who told you…?'

She couldn't go on. She felt hurt, bewildered—devastated. She'd known that Niall had been insecure. Possessive. Even unsure of her. But not to the degree that he'd have expressed his concerns to anyone else…

'Why would he have had reason to suspect you if it wasn't true?'

His brother's flaying demand shook her out of the numbing shock of what she had just learned.

'Because just like you he wouldn't accept that a man I cared about could be anything other than romantically involved with me,' she flung at him bitterly.

'*A man you cared about?*' he underscored derogatorily, a black winged eyebrow climbing his forehead.

'Make of it what you will!' she snapped, folding her arms and clutching her elbows tight in a totally defensive gesture against all he was saying.

'My brother obviously did.' Conan was giving her no quarter. 'Did you even realise how crazy he was about you?'

'Yes.'

'And what was wrong with that, Sienna? Does a man's loving you make him somehow less of a man in your eyes?'

'Of course not!'

'Just an inconvenience, then?'

'No!'

'Then what were you doing that morning in another man's flat—especially one you *cared* about—' his tone was censuring '—if you weren't having an affair?'

Relaxing her arms a little, she said pointedly, 'Would you believe just visiting him?'

Harsh scepticism touched his mouth. 'I might if it hadn't been so obvious that you'd been sleeping there. Or if you hadn't been so ready to lie to your husband about where you were going every time you went "shopping" for the day, dragging your toddler along with you to witness your illicit little affair. So why did you—*if* you're as innocent as you say you were? Answer me that.'

She couldn't. Even now, hurting as she was from his brother's suspicions, the reason why she had been with Timothy Leicester that night stayed locked inside her, incriminating her, giving her no leeway to explain herself—just as it had then, three years ago. But at least she could try to defend herself against something.

'I lied because I couldn't mention Tim's name without Niall getting unnecessarily upset,' she supplied, admitting that much at least.

'And you find that surprising?' Incredulity marked features bathed bronze in the evening sun. 'In the world I inhabit —and I think most conventional couples—the presence of an old boyfriend on the scene would spark off the same reaction in anyone who happened to be the slighted partner.'

'He wasn't slighted—and Tim wasn't my boyfriend!' she asserted in self-defence.

'That wasn't the general consensus of opinion amongst the people my investigative team spoke to.'

'You had me *investigated?*' she whispered, her nose wrinkling in disbelief. She couldn't believe that Niall had been so unsure of her as to let his brother do something so underhand.

'My own idea,' Conan stated coolly, uncannily aware of what she was thinking, if not of the turmoil going on inside of her. 'There were those who knew you and this Leicester character who swore the two of you were an item—made for each other. They were even surprised you hadn't got married. Neighbours. Friends. Old acquaintances. It paints a somewhat less innocuous picture of the two of you, don't you think?' he suggested derisively.

'Because they'd all wanted us to!' she exhaled, angry colour touching her cheeks. 'And you had absolutely no right to question my friends or anyone else I knew like that!'

'I had every right when I saw what you were doing to my brother,' he sliced back, offering no apology. 'But don't worry. Those in question wouldn't even have guessed that they were being interrogated, let alone that your whiter-than-white reputation was being put under scrutiny. So what do you have to say for yourself now, Sienna? Still think you can convince me he wasn't an old boyfriend?'

'Obviously not!' she snapped, realising it was hopeless even imagining she could. The evidence against her was far too damning. 'Think what you like,' she sighed wearily, turning away. 'If you don't believe me, then that's your problem. Not mine.'

Only it *was* her problem, she thought despairingly, because she was only just beginning to realise that for some reason beyond her comprehension what Conan Ryder thought of her mattered. It mattered a lot.

'All you've done is put two and two together and come up with nothing!' she tagged on, turning towards him again, and wishing she hadn't when she noticed how his eyes were glittering gold beneath the sinking sun, and how the wind was ruffling his sleek black hair. 'Which just goes to show how narrow-minded you are!' she accused, angry with herself for noticing. 'As well as bigoted, single-minded and mercenary!'

'Is that all?' Instead of the anger she'd expected her accusations to generate, a slow smile was curling his stupendous mouth. 'Perhaps we recognise these things in each other, Sienna? Which could account for why we're so attracted to each other.'

'You don't attract me.' As an attempt at a bare-faced lie, it was so crass as to be laughable.

'Don't I?' he queried silkily. 'I'd beg to dispute that.'

You stupid, stupid fool! Of *course* a man like Conan couldn't be held up to challenge, she thought. He thrived on challenges. Knew how to take them on and overcome them. And now because of her stupid big mouth she was going to have to face further humiliation. Because he was right. She was so attracted to him that if he so much as touched her...

She suddenly tensed as his arm snaked around the back of her seat, his long dark hand coming to rest on the contrasting paleness of the leather.

As he leaned across her she pressed herself back against the upholstery, hardly daring to breathe, yet found that the action had brought her into contact with the stirring warmth of his sleeve. She could feel the sensuality of the silk against the nape of her neck.

'Are you going to subdue me? Is that it?' she challenged shakily, her breathing so laboured it was difficult to speak.

He laughed very softly, his breath warm at her

temple, the action gently stirring her hair. 'You don't strike me as a woman who would take that sort of treatment from any man—least of all one whom you believe despises you. You're much too liberated—too self-assured—to play the subservient little sex-slave. I want you as an equal, Sienna,' he purred deeply, his face so close to hers that she closed her eyes to blot out those darkly alluring features, feeling his breath as a sensual caress against her lips. 'Which is how I want you to want me. Giving as much as you take.'

He had moved his arm slightly, so that he wasn't even touching her now, but his words and the tonal quality of his voice along with the tantalising scent of him was a turn-on such as she would never have believed.

For the first time in her life the thought of what she wanted to do to a man—and not just any man but to him—was an aphrodisiac greater than any she had ever known.

She wanted to hide how she felt, but her breasts were already betraying her. She felt their burgeoning sensitivity, gasping deeply as his warm hand brushed across one taut hard peak so fleetingly that she might have imagined it.

Tense, wanting, she tilted her face to his, crazy for the feel of his mouth on hers.

'Oh, I'm not going to kiss you, Sienna.'

Her eyes flew open—not only at his declaration but at the amazing degree of self-control with which he had spoken.

'That would give you the opportunity of accusing me of instigating it.'

She couldn't believe what he was saying, or how unaffected he seemed to be after the effortless way in which he had aroused her.

'Why not? You did,' she snapped, burning with humiliation.

Unperturbed, he moved back to his own side of the car, fully in command of himself—and of her—as he started the ignition.

'At least try being honest with yourself, Sienna,' he advised, glancing over his shoulder before pulling back onto the public highway. 'If not with me.'

'I didn't want this,' she murmured, realising that with that defeated little statement she had admitted what her body had already told him. That it was true. She did want him. And with a desperation that hurt.

'Don't worry,' he rasped, looking at her tight strained features, giving the car full throttle as he took the road into the craggy hills. 'It won't last for ever.'

* * *

She didn't see him the following day, or the day after that, since he'd flown back to London for a conference. She spent the leisurely hours enjoying some quality time with Daisy, playing frisbee with her and Shadow on the private shingle beach, and building a kind of fragile peace with Avril.

Trying to let bygones be bygones, she brought her up to date with her little granddaughter's life, showing her early snapshots that she had brought with her for the woman to keep, as well as more recent photos of Daisy that were still on her cell phone.

She even encouraged Niall's mother to take a short evening stroll with her through the villa's spectacular grounds. She felt that Avril's problems might be more than physical, intuitively sensing that the woman was suffering from some sort of depression. From her training and experience with the older and less able-bodied people who joined the specialised courses she ran at the gym, she knew the benefits that gentle exercise could have on a person's well-being.

Consequently, when she went to bed that second night she drifted off to sleep feeling as though her day had been worthwhile—but woke up the following morning with a pounding head and aching all over.

'Tell Madame Ryder I'd better not come anywhere near her today,' she instructed Claudette,
having sought her out in the villa's large modern
kitchen. 'I think I'm going down with something.
And keep Daisy occupied, will you?' she implored
the little maid, who looked more than happy to be
asked. 'I wouldn't want her to catch anything if
I'm contagious.'

By lunchtime she was feeling so groggy she decided to go back to bed, annoyed at having to give
in to sickness when she was never ill.

Some time during the afternoon Claudette came
up with a tall and vastly expensive-looking vase
of equally tall assorted flowers.

'From *madame,*' she informed Sienna, setting
the vase carefully down on the high circular table
that stood against the far wall, leaving Sienna surprised, though touched by the gesture.

Her room was above the terrace, and through
the open window she could hear Avril's muted
tones overlaid by Daisy's more eager and breathless ones. Shadow, loyal as always, was curled up
asleep at the bottom of her bed. Lulled by the animal's gentle breathing, she began to relax, willing
her aching body to let her sleep.

A sudden sound opened her eyes.

The dog was awake and alert. But not as awake

and alert as Conan appeared to be as he came in, dressed for business as always, though his dark jacket had been discarded and his tie was pulled loose, the top button of his shirt unfastened, allowing a glimpse of the deeply tanned skin beneath.

'I understand you're not feeling well?' he said, without any preamble.

From the pillows, her hair dishevelled, her cheeks unnaturally flushed, Sienna pulled a self-deprecating face. 'I'm sorry.' She hadn't heard him knock, although she imagined he would have, and realised that she must have dropped off after all. 'You've got enough on your hands without having two sick women to worry about. I'm sure I'll be up and about again tomorrow.'

He didn't say anything, but just came over to the bed and felt her forehead. His touch was light, though his palm was strong and cool, and even now, feeling as she did, Sienna felt her body respond to it in a way that made her blood surge—and made her ache even more.

'You're burning up,' he remarked, his thick winged brows drawing together.

'I think I've got some sort of bug,' she said painfully. Why, if she had to be ill in somebody else's house, did it have to be his?

'Is there anything I can get you?' He looked so

disgustingly healthy that Sienna couldn't imagine any virus or anything else ever daring to attack *him*. 'Do you need anything?'

She certainly didn't want him running around after her. Nor did she want his sympathy, she thought, silently fending off any suggestion of it. Not that he seemed to be offering any!

'Just for this to go.'

Fortunately Daisy came running in, scampering over to the bed and easing the inevitable tension coursing through Sienna. 'Mummy!' The little girl launched herself at her, her little arms going fiercely around Sienna's neck.

'I'm all right, darling. Mummy will be fine in a day or two.' She patted the adoring arms. 'You go with Uncle Conan.' Gently she disentangled herself from the affectionate embrace. 'We don't want you catching anything nasty, do we?' On her feet again, Daisy shook her head. 'Take her with you, will you?' she asked the man, blue eyes meeting green-gold over the little girl's bright, bouncy curls.

From a few feet away, he gave a nod of silent assent, before Daisy darted over to him.

'Mummy isn't well,' she informed him, clutching one strong lean hand and looking trustingly up at his darkly aloof features.

'Then we'll just have to leave Mummy to get better, won't we?' he suggested, smiling indulgently down at the little girl. And the surprising warmth in the deep voice together with the sight of that little hand in his made Sienna's throat clog with unexpected emotion.

'If there's anything you need...' guiding Daisy away, he turned in the doorway '...let Claudette know immediately,' he instructed.

Claudette. Not him, she thought wretchedly as he went out with Daisy skipping beside him. Then suddenly Shadow took it on himself to desert her too, and shot out through the gap in the closing door.

Surely she hadn't wanted Conan to stay? How *could* she have wanted him to stay? she railed at herself, realising that she had. She could only justify the feeling by putting it down to the virus, which was obviously making her think irrationally, had her taking it to heart because he hadn't.

But how could a man as cold and heartless as Conan Ryder—except with Daisy of course—possibly sympathise with anyone who was ill? Especially someone he believed was as money-grubbing and deceitful as he thought she was.

A fact confirmed when he didn't return for the rest of the day—or the evening.

Claudette came up with Daisy for the little girl to give Sienna a goodnight kiss before going to bed, Shadow following at her heels. Even Avril sent up some of her best cranberry juice and a get-well wish through another servant, but there was no further sign of Conan.

Telling herself she didn't care one way or the other, Sienna tried to settle down. But her aches were getting worse, and despite the warm night she couldn't stop shivering—which meant she couldn't sleep, which in turn meant that she couldn't get Conan's cold indifference to her out of her mind.

It wasn't helped by the knowledge that he wouldn't hesitate to take her to bed if the opportunity arose, which just confirmed what a hard and unfeeling louse he was.

But she'd known that already. So why was she feeling so disappointed in him? she berated herself, screwing up her face with the aches that seemed to be gnawing at her body. She wasn't, she told herself belligerently, through her restless, groaning fever. Unable to bear feeling so grotty any longer, she broke her rule never to resort to medication and took two paracetamol—which someone had left on the bedside cabinet with Avril's cranberry juice—after which her bone-deep aches began to subside.

She awoke while it was still dark, drenched to the skin, her nightdress sticking to her like a wet sheet.

It *was* the sheet, she realised, dismayed, trying to kick it off her legs, where it clung, unpleasantly clammy and cold.

Obviously taking the painkillers had reduced her temperature, she thought, which meant having to suffer this side-effect instead.

Grateful, though, that she wasn't aching any more, she slipped out of bed and into the *en suite* bathroom without putting on the light—which had been all right when she'd had some light filtering up from the grounds through the bathroom's frosted window. But someone must have drawn the curtains in the bedroom while she'd slept, she realised, after she'd shut off that only source of light, and she found herself having to grope her way back across the luxurious Indian rug, so damp she was already starting to shiver. She couldn't see a thing, and she needed to find a dry nightdress—fast!

Her clothes had been unpacked for her on the day she had arrived, and her nightwear and underclothes were all neatly folded, drowning in the space provided by an endless array of drawers. But not altogether *au fait* with her surroundings, feeling her way in the dark, she stepped off the carpet onto the richness of wood—and misjudged exactly where she was, colliding with the table where Claudette had placed the heavy vase of flowers earlier in the day, sending it crashing to the floor.

'Oh, *no!*'

Her legs were splashed from the water, and desperately she groped for a light switch—only to find herself blinking by the illuminated landing as the door burst open a few seconds later, and her own room was flooded with light.

'What the…?'

It was Conan who stood there, holding the door wide, his face an orchestra of emotions from surprise and concern to outright disbelief.

'I'm sorry.' It was all Sienna could say, seeing his gaze slip from her dishevelled state to the shattered pieces of vase lying on the floor. 'Was it very expensive?'

'Never mind about that,' he told her. 'What are you doing wandering about in the dark? And what the…?'

She must look terrible, she thought wretchedly, seeing his gaze raking over her, with her hair a tangled mess and about as glamorous as a compost heap, while he…

Only now did it sink in that he must have been

undressing when he had heard the crash, because he was standing in nothing but the shirt he had been wearing earlier that day, which was fully unbuttoned and hanging open over a pair of dark briefs.

In normal circumstances she wouldn't have been able to take her eyes off that bronze, muscular chest, with its shading of black hair that arrowed down over his tight flat abdomen. Any more than she could have ignored the powerful thighs which, planted firmly apart and covered in the same fine hair, shouted of everything that was utterly virile and masculine. But her strappy nightdress was clinging to her feverish skin like cold wet polythene and her teeth were starting to chatter.

'I wanted a dry nightdress,' she was trying to say, but couldn't get it out because she was shivering so much.

'For goodness' sake!' In a few short strides he was beside her, and, having sussed the situation, was tugging at the offending garment. 'Take this thing off!'

She started to protest, but he was already ripping it over her head, so that she was left standing naked in front of him, covered by nothing except her goose pimples.

'This isn't the time for modesty—unless you

want to catch your death,' he advised, his mouth firming grimly. 'Here.' Having tossed the night-dress aside, he was shrugging out of his shirt, revealing his beautiful torso in all its glory. 'Put this on.'

Obediently Sienna slipped her arms into the silky fabric he was holding up for her. It felt warm and incredibly soft as she clutched her own arms, hugging its warmth to her, shuddering. Grateful. It smelt nice too. Like him. Lemony, tinged with spice, and somewhere in the mix a hint of musk...

'Now.' He had her by the elbow and was urging her back to bed, his other hand pulling back the covers. 'Get back in and—' He stopped mid-sentence, feeling the damp crumpled sheet. 'You can't sleep in that!' he remonstrated.

Before she realised it he had scooped her up into his arms. 'We've got to get you warm,' he insisted, ignoring her protests.

It was a miracle, Sienna thought distractedly, that Daisy hadn't been disturbed by all the commotion. She tried to ignore the feel of that warm, solid wall of muscle that she was being held against as Conan bore her down the landing to another room.

His bedroom! she realised at once, with her heart racing, seeing the enormous bed with its dark satin sheets, only half aware of the exclusive wood and the dark rich array of soft furnishings that defined it as very much a man's domain.

This time when he ripped back the sheet for her to climb in, he slipped quickly in beside her. Then, turning her onto her side with her back to him, he pulled her shivering body into the warm hard length of his.

She knew she should object—put up some resistance to his taking control like this. But she needed him right at this moment, and his body was so warm…

Even through her fogged senses she recognised a deep sensuality, but she blotted it out of her mind, letting the warmth of him ease and comfort her, penetrate her shuddering body.

Her breathing was rapid and shallow from the virus, but gradually it slowed and became steadier as her shivers began to subside.

She felt sleepy and so…protected.

It was a half-conscious thought, so transient she didn't even question the strangeness of it as she drifted off, secure in the strength of his arms and in the cushioning warmth of his body.

CHAPTER SIX

WHEN she awoke she was alone.

Only the depression in the pillow beside hers assured her that she hadn't dreamt the whole thing. Plus the fact that she was still in his room—and in his bed! she realised with a self-ridiculing little grimace.

Surprisingly, though, she felt considerably better.

But where was he? And, more importantly, where was Daisy?

As her maternal instincts kicked in she scrambled out of bed, and was halfway across the room before she realised that she was still wearing Conan's shirt. The shirt he had helped her into after stripping her naked! The shirt she had been too shivery and unwell last night even to fasten!

Hearing a sudden soft knock on the door, she raced back to bed, only just managing to cover herself with the dark maroon sheet before the door opened and Claudette came in.

'Monsieur Ryder's instructions,' she declared in

her heavily accented voice as she set a breakfast tray down on a marble-topped coffee table.

There was a jug of orange juice, and coffee in a silver pot, its aroma drifting tantalisingly towards Sienna. There were croissants too, she noticed, still warm from the oven, their buttery, freshly baked smell making her mouth water.

She was hungry, she realised, after eating scarcely anything the previous day.

'Claudette? Where's Daisy?'

The little maid paused in pouring juice into a crystal tumbler. 'I am not sure, *madame*. She had breakfast with Madame Ryder an hour ago, but I think Monsieur Ryder's taken her out with him.'

Without consulting her, or bringing Daisy up here to see her mother first? Sienna thought, stunned, wondering what could possibly have prompted such an action on Conan's part when he seemed to have had very little time for his niece since she had been there. Nevertheless, she couldn't help feeling that her role as guardian was being undermined.

'Oh…' she uttered, and hoped she didn't sound as hurt or put out as she felt.

'Is there anything else I can get you, *madame?*' Claudette asked helpfully as she finished rearranging things on the tray.

'No. Thank you,' Sienna said, embarrassed by

what the woman must be thinking about finding Monsieur Ryder's sick young guest in Monsieur Ryder's bed. 'Oh—yes. Claudette…!'

The little maid was already on her way out.

'Do you think you could bring me some clothes?' She felt sticky and sweaty and she was longing for a shower. But she had no intention of risking anyone else in the house seeing her emerge from Monsieur Ryder's bedroom wearing only Monsieur Ryder's shirt!

'Oui, madame.'

The woman was back in minutes with fresh underwear, a casual check shirt and jeans, which she placed tidily over the wooden arm of a richly upholstered gold brocade chair.

'Shoes, too,' she said, placing them beside the bed, where Sienna was sitting with the sheet still pulled up around her, in a rather futile bid to conceal her betraying appearance.

Claudette was looking pleased with herself, as if she did this sort of thing all the time.

Which perhaps she did, Sienna thought suddenly, biting into one of the warm, moist croissants, wondering why the thought of Conan entertaining other women like this should bother her in quite the way it did. Women like Petra Flax.

'Claudette…' Wiping crumbs from the corner

of her mouth, Sienna tried to imagine what reason Conan might have given his employee for Sienna being in his bed. In case he hadn't said anything, she felt she needed to put the record straight.

Now, though, as the woman waited for her to continue, Sienna merely shrugged. It was too complicated to try and explain.

After the maid had gone, she ravenously ate two of the croissants, finished her juice and a cup of coffee, and then, as Conan was clearly not around, took advantage of the facilities of his bathroom.

It was of a similar design to hers, though the long luxurious bath and the rest of the gleaming white suite was enhanced by a colour scheme of sage and dark green marble.

The sensuously appointed double shower was something she tried not to think about too much as she luxuriated in the steaming water from its powerful jets, while soaping her hair and her body with his citrus-fragranced shower gel.

Claudette hadn't thought to bring her a robe, so she grabbed Conan's when she'd finished, finding it hanging behind the door—a thick, white towelling garment that seemed to swamp her in its folds, and carried the disturbing and far too evocative scent of his body.

She was aching to see Daisy, though, and made

short work of towelling her hair, needing to get downstairs and quiz her mother-in-law over where Conan had gone—and where he had taken his niece without *her* permission.

Standing in front of the mirrored wardrobe, teasing her hair into some semblance of order, she was trying to decide what she was going to say to him about it, particularly after he had rescued her from what would have been a very uncomfortable night, when the bedroom door suddenly creaked open just a crack—and then enough to allow a little grinning figure to scamper in.

'Daisy!'

Sienna's heart lurched as she swept her daughter up into her arms. 'Oh, goodness! I've missed you!' She was hugging and kissing her as though she hadn't seen her daughter for months, breathing in her infant scent, revelling in the feel of her warm, familiarly solid little body.

'I got Uncle Conan to take me out 'cause my green crayon's all gone.' She spilled the words out, punctuating the statement with little breaths. 'Because you were asleep and no one else wanted to take me.'

'I expect they were busy, darling,' Sienna told her gently, trying to control her surprise as she stroked the soft chestnut hair.

'Uncle Conan told me to give you these.' Giving her some space at last, Sienna realised that the little girl was clutching a small bouquet of gaily coloured flowers. A couple of the heads were crushed from the ferocity of her affection, she noticed, sending a glance down at the crimson smudge staining the pristine whiteness of Conan's robe. 'He said you dropped all the ones Granny gave you.'

'Oh, darling…' Restraining a sob, taking the flowers from the small hand, Sienna hugged Daisy to her again—and only then became aware of Conan in a light, stylishly tailored suit, leaning with his arms folded against the doorjamb.

'We looked in earlier but you were asleep,' he said, straightening up to his impressive height and moving towards them. 'I thought you might have wanted to take Daisy yourself, but decided it best to let you sleep on.'

'Thanks,' Sienna uttered, ashamed to realise she had misjudged him, yet amazed that he had involved himself in something so trivial as a child's crayons. 'You didn't mind taking her?'

He shrugged, as though it was of little consequence, but didn't say whether he had or not. In fact he hadn't wanted to get drawn in at all. But when he had told the little girl that her mother wasn't well enough to take her out, and to use a different colour, she'd declared quite adamantly that grass could only be green, stamped her foot, and started to cry.

'Like most members of her sex, she knows just how to manipulate,' he commented dryly, and only that touch of humour on his lips stopped Sienna from coming back with some suitable retort. Not to mention that her body was responding to his impeccably tailored elegance and those deeply stunning features in a way that was far, far too disturbing!

'I take it you're feeling better?'

'Yes. Thanks,' she murmured, just the memory of how he had stripped her of that wet nightdress and carried her in here causing wings of colour to deepen across her cheeks. 'You were very kind.'

He laughed—a rather dispassionate sound. 'That's the first time anyone's ever accused me of that.'

Because "kind" didn't really seem to fit a man like Conan Ryder, Sienna thought, and the polite smile she gave him—like his laugh just now—was a little bit strained.

Hard, tough and practical. Those were the adjectives she would use to describe the man standing in front of her, she decided, setting Daisy down on her feet as soon as she started to wriggle.

'Uncle Conan?' With her hippo under her arm, she ran over to the man she seemed hell-bent on winning over, whether he liked it or not, grabbing one of his impeccably clad legs. 'Are you going to marry Mummy?'

Sienna, horrified, heard her.

Conan's forehead pleated in a kind of amused perplexity.

'Why on earth,' he said, with a curious edge to his voice, 'do you ask that?'

'She's in *your* bedroom.' The child looked coyly at her mother, as though she knew it was a subject that only adults should talk about. 'And she's got your dressing gown on.'

Conan's mouth pulled wryly as he glanced across at Sienna. 'So she has!' he declared, as though he had only just noticed.

His eyes were lingering on the swamping garment, which on him would probably only cover his thighs, Sienna thought, and a flood of warmth heated her body at the memory of those virile thighs and just how he had looked when he had carried her in here last night.

But now he was fully clothed, and as devastating to her equilibrium as when he had been nearly naked. Particularly when those perceptive eyes were raking over her as they were now, taking in the rolled-back sleeves and the gaping neckline of the robe, which she had only just realised was revealing far too much of the upper swell of one breast, and which her agitated fingers struggled to rectify.

'Why don't you go down and show your grand-mother the new colouring book we chose this morning?' he suggested to his niece. 'I'm sure she'd like to see you using your new crayons. I'll send your mother down to join you as soon as she's ready.'

Phew!

Sienna's relief was palpable as the little girl did as he advised and scampered away.

'Thanks,' she said again, placing the flowers down on the table, envying the way he appeared so unfazed by the child's remarks.

'All in a day's work.' The line of his mouth curved sensuously, sending Sienna's already hope-less defences against him skittering like a retreat-ing army. 'Does she always carry that hippo with her?' he asked, with a jerk of his chin towards the door he had just closed.

'She won't be parted from it,' she murmured unthinkingly, suddenly nervous at finding herself alone with him.

A line deepened between those thick masculine brows, and his gaze was so intense it felt as though he was probing right down into her soul and sussing out that she hadn't really wanted to tell him that. That the simple gift he'd bought for his niece's first birthday had eclipsed any other toy she'd ever been given.

She hadn't played with it at first, Sienna remembered. It had been just one more of the large number of cuddly toys that had filled Daisy's bedroom. In fact she'd scarcely noticed it for six months—not until after Niall had died. Then she had plucked it up one day and ever afterwards clung to it like a lifeline, taking it to bed, to playschool, wherever else she went, as though it somehow represented all the love and support and comfort that her father's absence had robbed her of. But Sienna couldn't bring herself to tell Conan any of that.

Now, trying to diminish the significance of what she had said, in case he read far too much into it, she shrugged, adding nonchalantly, 'Well, you know children. They go through these phases, don't they?'

'I don't know,' he said, in a surprisingly cool tone. 'I've never had any.'

For one crazy moment she had the strongest urge to ask him if he ever wanted any, but decided that that was a subject she didn't want to pursue with him either—particularly as he sounded less than enamoured of the idea.

'I'll get dressed and leave you to it,' she murmured, moving over to the chair where Claudette had left her clothes.

'Don't rush on my account,' he said dispassionately, turning away.

The bathroom beckoned. Privacy. A place where she could get dressed and then get out of there as smartly as she could. Except that her gaze moved too willingly towards where he was standing, with his back to her now, rummaging through one of the drawers, and she couldn't for the life of her tear it away.

Greedily her eyes ran over the wide sweep of his shoulders, tapered to perfection by the exclusive cut of his jacket, to his narrow waist and long, long legs. Very masculine legs that had rasped against hers as he'd warmed her in his bed. Even through her fever she had been mind-blowingly aware of him, had known that in any other circumstances she couldn't have lain with him like that, feeling the power of his arms and the rousing warmth of his body, without turning towards him…

And he would have taken her.

Gathering up her clothes, she felt her blood surge at the memory. He had shown care and concern and overall commitment for her welfare, but he hadn't been able to conceal the physical evidence of his wanting her...

But he *had* shown that care—and to a woman he didn't even like. She was his least favourite person and yet he had held her through the night...

Trying to puzzle him out, her clothes clutched tightly to her, she heard the question that had been burning through her brain ever since she'd woken up this morning slip out before she could stop it. 'Why didn't you help Niall when he asked you to?'

The drawer closing hard on its runners was the only sound to intrude on the pregnant silence that followed. 'I had my reasons,' he replied, moving back across the room.

'What reasons?' Sienna persisted, swivelling to look at him as he crossed over to the wardrobe. 'What reason could be good enough for not helping your own brother? For just standing by while he got into such unavoidable debt?'

'Unavoidable?' With an eyebrow raised censoriously, he shot a glance in her direction.

Tension spread through Sienna's body. He thought *she* had been responsible for most of it.

'All right, then,' he rasped, taking a coat hanger out of the wardrobe. 'If you want to know the truth. I did help him.'

'You did?'

'At least, I tried to.'

'What do you mean?' she asked, screwing her face up.

'Where do you think the money came from for your fancy house, Sienna? For a large part of his investments? The back-up? The loans?'

'But I thought—'

'You thought what? What you've always thought?' He tossed the hanger down on a chair and started shrugging out of his jacket. 'That I left my own brother to stew?'

'But Niall said—'

'I'm well aware of what Niall must have said. And, yes, all right. That's how it must have looked,' he accepted, retrieving the hanger. 'As though I was a heartless bastard.'

Which was exactly what Niall had called him, Sienna remembered.

'Then why did he say it if it wasn't true?' Niall might have had his shortcomings, but he certainly hadn't been a liar, she thought, watching him hanging up his jacket.

'Because I did refuse him.' He was closing the wardrobe door. 'Later.'

'Why?'

'You won't like it, Sienna.'

She watched him move over to the table and drop his keys down beside the bouquet Daisy had given her. 'Because of me?'

He didn't answer. He didn't have to. His silence made it all too plain.

'I was sick of funding your lifestyle because Niall didn't have the gumption to control it. Any more than he had the commitment or the dedication for directorship.'

'That isn't true! I never asked him for anything! The car. The clothes. Every expensive gift he bought me!' Nothing had been too good for her, she remembered, with a surge of painful emotion pressing heavily against her chest, although she'd tried to dissuade him from spending so much, concerned about the cost. 'Niall worked hard,' she reminded Conan, because his brother *had* always been working. Using that unique Ryder charm on clients to secure deals. Striving to make himself as rich and respected and as successful as Conan was. Sometimes, she thought now, it had been almost painful watching him. 'He worked *hard*,' she reiterated. 'You know he did!

'But he spent more than he earned, Sienna.'

'So you decided to pull the plug? Because you thought I was the one spending it all?'

From the anguish scoring her face, he was almost willing to believe that she was telling him the truth. That she really didn't have a clue what had been going on. But whether she had or not, it didn't alter the fact that she was still a cheat...

'When I did have a change of heart and decided to throw him a lifeline he wouldn't even speak to me,' he informed her, the memory eating at him. Because however different their lives had been, or how diverse their characters, there had been an unbreakable bond between them, forged out of Niall's eternal yet unconscious need for guidance, and out of his own responsibility as the elder brother to see that he got it. 'I tried again—several times—even ringing him when he wouldn't see me, but he cut me dead on every occasion. Told me he'd sorted it out for himself.'

Which he had, Sienna thought. By mortgaging a house which, she was staggered to realise now, Conan had paid for. By securing extortionately priced loans she'd suddenly found herself responsible for. And for what? she wondered bitterly.

'Why didn't you tell me before?' she murmured distantly, clinging to the bundle of clothes she was holding like a shield. 'Three years ago?'

'What would it have achieved, Sienna?' he enquired resignedly. 'Absolution for myself at the expense of my brother's reputation?' The brother he'd always felt duty-bound to protect—from himself, if nothing else, he thought grimly. He had recognised his brother's weakness even from an early age. 'Especially when his grieving widow had only just emerged from another man's bed?'

Wearily, she said, 'It wasn't like that.'

'No, of course not.' He laughed humourlessly, refusing to believe her. Just as he had three years ago. Although he was unburdening himself, she thought, without any problem! 'Apart from which,' he went on, 'I didn't think Niall would have considered I was doing him any favours by telling his wife just how much financial support his brother had given him.'

'Then why are you telling me now?'

He was moving towards her with a purposefully predatory stride, stopping only when he was breath-catching inches away from her. 'I think you know why.'

Yes, I do! she thought, weakened by his nearness, by his unmistakable scent that did things to her like no other man's had ever done, and by the mesmerising gold of his eyes.

Directed only by his will, she allowed him to take the small bundle of clothes she was clutching and drop them onto the chair, his eyes never leaving hers. She wondered if he could hear the way her heart was banging against her ribcage.

Her breath shuddered through her at those galvanising fingers against the nape of her neck. His hand curled around her, drawing her closer, and with her breath coming shallowly, she closed her eyes, her head dropping back of its own volition, her mouth tilted upwards to his.

His kiss was light, gentle, considered, bearing none of the demanding hunger he had shown in the pool. But his tenderness was torment and, made brave by the way he had treated her last night, and by the unbelievable things she had just learned about him, she slid her arms around his neck with a little murmur of acquiescence, wanting this as she had never wanted anything in her life.

He responded with an iron-strong arm around her middle, pulling her against the whipcord strength of his body.

Her own actions had loosened the belt of the bulky robe. She wasn't aware of it until his hand slid inside the parting garment, and she gave a throaty gasp as, with both hands sliding down to her hips, he pulled her against the rock-hard thrust of his masculinity.

The friction of his clothes was an aphrodisiac against her bare flesh, bringing her wriggling against him in involuntary provocation as each movement opened up a sensual heaven.

Her breasts were begging for his attention, their swollen peaks tightening into hard buds. With a small whimper she thrust them out to him in mindless invitation, flaunting her femininity before him with all the shamelessness of an abandoned nymph.

With the proficiency of a master, he read her body's silent language, drawing his tongue teasingly down the silken valley between her aching breasts, and chuckling softly at her stifled little groan of need.

One hand sliding under each breast, he cupped them as if they were prize roses, making her wait as he studied them with those darkly penetrating eyes, making her ache for him, making her silently beg.

Very gently he dipped his head to suckle first on one and then the other, tasting each sensitive tip before exploring the pink halo around it with his tongue.

His breath was unbearably sensual as it fanned the burning tip of each pale mound, increasing her pleasure with the cooling dew of his saliva, his actions slow and studied, exquisitely arousing, excruciatingly erotic.

Only it wasn't enough…

Sensations shuddered through her, sending shock-waves of pure pleasure right down to the aching heart of her femininity, the sensual message they carried clear and unequivocal.

She wanted him! Wanted him as she had never wanted any man. Wanted to be in bed with him as she had been last night—only without restraint and without the barrier of any clothes between them.

He didn't like her. But she would *make* him like her, she vowed to her own shocked consciousness, although that didn't matter now. All that mattered was that he wanted her as much as she wanted him. Driven by her need, she ground her hips sensuously against the hard structure of his and heard him groan with the agony of his own need.

Her hands were running over the fine silk of his shirt, exploring the warm contours of his chest, his flanks, and the hard straining muscles of his back.

She wanted to be naked with him. To feel his body slick and hot against hers. But as she started pulling awkwardly at the front of the immaculate shirt he slammed his hand over hers, holding it flat against his chest.

She could hear the thunder of his heart beneath her fingers, and there were slashes of dark colour along the sculpted lines of his cheeks. His eyelids were heavy, his eyes darkened by desire, but with

a soft chuckle that was at odds with the ragged-
ness of his breathing, he murmured, 'You aren't
well enough for this.'

He was lifting her up, carrying her over to the
big bed just as he had done last night. Only now,
as she reached out to him, lying with her body
unashamedly exposed to him by the gaping robe,
it was only his dark-fringed eyes that caressed
her supple nakedness, before he straightened and
moved away from the bed.

A small moan of disappointment escaped her.

She couldn't believe it! He was picking up the
phone on the bedside unit.

How could he be making a phone call at a time
like this? she wondered through a mire of frustration, even if he *did* think he was being considerate
in calling a halt to their lovemaking? Had he only
been teasing her? Setting her alight only to douse
the fire he had ignited with his disciplined self-
control? And if so, why? Because he didn't like
her? she thought despairingly. Because of what
she still couldn't convince him she hadn't done?

'Yes, it's me,' she heard him say into the mouthpiece of what she realised then was the internal
phone. 'Keep Daisy with you for a while, will
you?' The phone pinged as he dropped it back onto
its rest.

Aching with frustration, an arm flung out across the bedspread, her aroused body given added voluptuousness by the gaping robe, Sienna still couldn't believe it as she watched him stride across the room without so much as a glance in her direction—until, with a wild leap of her pulse, she heard him locking the door.

'Now…' he murmured, his mouth taking on an excitingly sensual twist as he turned back to where she was lying. 'Are you going to convince me that you are?'

CHAPTER SEVEN

COMING back across the room, Conan could feel his arousal straining against his trousers.

If Sienna was trying to test his restraint, he observed grimly, she was doing a very good job!

She was lying on her back with her legs drawn up to one side, with his robe covering only her arms and part of one shoulder like a pale frame for the soft lines and curves of her delicious body.

He guessed she was well aware of how tempting she looked. And if she wasn't, then she was certainly going to find out, he resolved, with a hard excitement throbbing through the lower half of his anatomy.

He allowed himself to take in the visual spectacle of all she was offering him. Skin like silk, from her lovely face and that natural complexion—paler today than it usually was—right down to her tantalisingly pink-tipped toes.

Her breasts were rising and falling sharply as he

came and stood over her, their equally tantalising pink crests still swollen from his ministrations.

He restrained the strongest urge to spread his hands across them. Going for the erogenous zones first never had been his style, and he had never been a man to rush things if he could help it. Besides, he enjoyed the art of titillation and reward. It heightened experience, and in the lifetime of his sexual maturity he had never had any complaints.

Her breathing seemed to quicken as his gaze slid down her body.

Surprisingly embarrassed, she made to draw her legs up further, and gave a little murmur—a token of protest—as he took a slender foot in each hand to swivel her round, pulling her gently towards him with her legs a little way off the bed so that he could position himself standing between them.

Her body was so enticing that the throbbing in his loins became almost unbearable. Her waist was remarkably slim beneath those proportionately full breasts, her hips an inviting cradle above the apex of her thighs and the dark downy hair covering the very centre of her.

The silky triangle drew his gaze to the slick, secret haven of her femininity, and he allowed his

eyes to linger there for a few moments before lifting his eyes to hers again and enjoying the flush
of colour he could see staining her cheeks.

When she moved to pull the robe together he
laughed and, bending over her, caught her hands,
holding them fast in one of his so that he could continue his inspection, aware from her soft groan and
her slumberous blue eyes that she was as aroused
as he was.

Had his brother wanted her like this? Been driven
mad by that body and that treacherously seductive
mouth? he wondered, sliding his forefinger across
its lower lip, feeling its inner warmth as her mouth
parted to admit him, cushioning him—mimick-
ing that ultimate act. Just as anticipating her sur-
render was driving *him* insane with wanting now?

Had *he* wanted her this much then too? Three?
Four? Five years ago? he asked himself almost sav-
agely, his mood incongruous with his actions as he
drew his moistened finger with considered gentle-
ness down the silken valley between her breasts.
Was that why he had kept his distance from her?
Why he hadn't wanted to believe Niall when he'd
told him he suspected her of having an affair?

The purposefulness with which he pulled off his
tie, tossing it aside before unbuttoning his shirt,
reflected the grim path his thoughts had taken.

Because the discovery that she was, and that she'd just been using his brother, had at the time rocked him like a tidal wave—especially in view of what had happened to Niall.

But now, as she reached for him, he realised he was just as much in danger of succumbing to her charms as his younger brother had been. Except that he was harder than Niall and far, far more experienced. Experienced enough never to let that happen. Because she was his now by tacit assent, to do whatever he liked with.

Which was to take her and take her until she screamed with the pleasure of it, he realised, hating himself even as his body hardened in scorching response to the thought of having her pleading and begging for him to end the pleasurable torture as he drove them both beyond ecstasy—before he walked away from her without batting an eyelid, letting her know exactly how it felt to be used.

Dragging his shirt down over his shoulders, Sienna allowed him to help her. Her fingers were clumsy—too eager—and fleetingly she wondered how the more sophisticated women of his acquaintance—and especially the likes of Petra Flax—would behave.

But the velvet-sheathed steel of his body drove her negative thoughts from her mind. He was with her, wasn't he? And even if this summer was all there was ever going to be with him she could accept that, couldn't she? A casual affair? People did. Other women she knew did it all the time.

'Conan…' She breathed his name like a reverent prayer, exalted by the way it felt on her lips, by being able to use it in such a way, like a coveted possession, something only granted to the favoured few.

Although probably more than a few, she thought with a mental grimace as she considered how many women might have sobbed out their pleasure on this same big bed. But she didn't want to dwell on that.

She wanted to explore him, and she used her hands and her lips to make her intentions known, luxuriating in the strength of him as her teeth lightly grazed over the hard, undulating contours of a sinewy arm, and her fingers revelled in the pelt of hair that shadowed his deep bronzed chest.

'Turn over,' she breathed, thrilled and a bit overawed by his glorious masculinity.

He laughed softly, doing as she asked.

She looked at him as he lay on his back with his eyes closed, his lashes thick and dark against the wells of his eyes, his hard mouth curving slightly, sensually relaxed.

Delicately she touched the tip of her tongue to his chest, letting it burn a trail over the dark line of hair that went down and down and disappeared under the waistband of his trousers, her senses imbued with his musky scent, the sound of his quickened breathing, and the salty taste of his skin.

'Are you going to take them off?' she suggested. Her hands were dealing with the buttons at his waist, her eyes bright with devilish excitement.

'I was hoping you were,' he drawled, his smile equally wicked.

Was he?

A little skein of excitement began unravelling inside of her.

He was hers to do with as she wanted. This big, important man with hidden depths to his character such as she hadn't realised until last night—and then again with that startling revelation this morning. She felt like a kid who had just been given a pomegranate and wasn't really sure what to do with it. Which was crazy, she thought, when she had been married for two and a half years! But then Niall had never encouraged her to take any initiative in their lovemaking. He'd always wanted to be in control, setting the pace and the rhythm. He'd wanted her submissive as he'd lost himself in her body. Idolising. Adoring. Dominating her...

Shaking the memory away, she slipped the zip down over the bulging fabric with surprisingly trembling fingers, as nervous as a schoolgirl on her first date.

'Do you usually let your women undress you?' she enquired, not wanting to imagine anyone else doing what she was doing to him, although she couldn't help it. Somehow she couldn't see Petra Flax feeling as gauche and awkward as she felt.

'That's none of your business,' he remonstrated softly, smiling at her cheekiness.

No, it wasn't, she thought, approving of him not telling her. He would be as discreet about his bedroom adventures as he was about the rest of his personal life.

'You're going to have to help me,' she said shyly.

'Really?' He was lying indolently on his back, and his face was a study in desire, from his heavy-lidded eyes and the flush staining the dark olive of his skin, to his full lower lip that was curling almost mockingly now. 'You disappoint me,' he said, before making quick work of dispensing with the hampering garment—and although Sienna knew he was only joking she felt his wry amusement like a shaming reprimand.

'Lie back,' she ordered, her heart fluttering nervously in her chest.

He was wearing little more than a black pouch that scarcely contained his manhood.

Sienna ran her hand lovingly across it, letting her palm size the dark bulk that was the most intimate part of his body. She gave him a self-satisfied smile, getting her own back when she heard the pleasurable groan that came from deep in his throat.

'I'll teach you to laugh at me,' she breathed, enjoying this sensual game with him that was thrilling and unexplored and totally new to her.

'Please do,' he murmured, his sexy mouth curling with wry anticipation, although his eyes were closed and his forehead crumpled in almost pained compliance.

Conan compliant! She almost laughed at the incongruity of it. Like a sleeping lion more like! she thought, considering the strength and power that could spring into action in a second, and a small frisson sizzled through her at the realisation that it was only the power of what she was doing to him that was keeping him still.

When she pulled down the last barrier—the only thing separating her from him—she closed her eyes and let her nervous hands caress him. He felt so hot and hard.

Emboldened by his groans of pleasure, she bent her head to taste him.

At the first touch of her mouth he shuddered violently against her, the power of his body arousing her in such a way as she'd never known she could be aroused from doing this to a man. Gently she used her breath to fan him, as he had done so expertly to her earlier across her aching breasts.

But, untutored in such a highly intimate game, she let her nerves get the better of her, and suddenly unready, feeling grossly inept with a man of such sexual prowess, she was murmuring like a fool before she could stop herself, 'I've never done this before.' She couldn't even look at him as she said it. She had never wanted to, she admitted to herself, feeling the dark clouds of her inadequacy threatening her, just as they had in her marriage. Not once, she remembered. Not until now...

She heard his breath shiver through him.

'Look at me,' he ordered deeply.

The eyes that met his when she raised herself up seemed guarded and... What? Conan wondered. Embarrassed? he considered, surprised. There was no doubt in his mind that she was telling him the truth.

So her previous sexual exploits, even in her marriage, hadn't included such adventurous intimacies, he realised with increasing surprise. Even though adultery had.

His grim acceptance of that, despite her continual denial, still couldn't diminish the rather chauvinistic pleasure of knowing that there was at least something left that he could teach her. But not today…

Her slender hand was resting on the flat plane of his abdomen.

Reaching down and clasping it in the lean strength of his, he said tonelessly, 'Maybe now isn't the time.'

A thin line appeared between finely shaped eyebrows.

Maybe it never would be, Sienna thought, wondering if her failure to please him meant he wouldn't want such an unsophisticated female in his bed again.

Desperate to do something that would keep him there, she marked a trail of butterfly kisses over the firm bed of his abdomen, her tongue lightly following where her lips had caressed, drawing a map of his body from his waist, down over his hip, from the sleekness of his skin to a thin, rough protrusion of flesh…

She sat up, staring at the jagged maroon line that

ran diagonally across the outer side of his right thigh.

'Where did you get that scar?' Scars, she amended silently, noticing now that there were some smaller ones further up along his hipbone.

She could feel the tension that was suddenly flexing his powerful body, as though he had taken a breath and forgotten to let it out.

'Let's just say I had a difference of opinion with one of our canine friends,' he said dispassionately, releasing air from his lungs again.

'A difference…? You mean these are dog bites? How? When?' Sienna asked, horrified, running cool fingers caressingly across his flesh as though she could erase whatever had caused them.

'I was somewhere I shouldn't have been—and I paid the price for it.' Twice over, he remembered grimly. He didn't know what had been worse. The violent attack by that savage Doberman, or his stepfather's… A curtain came down over his thoughts, swiftly blotting out the memory. 'It was a long time ago.'

A long time ago, and yet he still bore the scars both mentally and physically, he reflected, quietly seething. And the reminder of that time, along with a sudden conscience-pricking thought as to what he was doing with his brother's little tramp of a widow, acted like a dousing of icy water over his skin.

'Conan…?'

As he lay there for a moment, trying to regain his zeal, her soft, enquiring whisper was all it took to pull him back.

And why not? he asked himself ruthlessly, moving as swiftly as a cat, hauling her up against him, before rolling them both so that she was lying beneath him. If anyone could help him wipe out his past then she could, he thought. Surprising though it was, she had the power in her small slender body and her contesting little opinions to excite him like no other woman had ever done.

She gave a deep moan of pleasure at the weight of him above her, her mouth as insistent as his as it parted for him in a mutual blending of searching tongues.

Her skin was soft and damp as he blazed a trail of urgent kisses down over her throat to the invitingly soft mounds of her breasts. He wanted to pour out his pent-up emotions against them. Take solace in the warm haven of her femininity. But how could a girl like her sympathise with the torments of his childhood? Or understand the demons that were riding him now?

She gave a soft whimper as though she was hurting and he raised himself up on his elbows. She was lying against the pillow, her beautiful eyes dark with desire, but her tousled hair was damp where it kinked around her temples, and there was an unnaturally high flush to the fine translucency of her cheeks.

What was he *doing?* he demanded of himself—though for a different reason this time. She looked all in, he thought. Exhausted, fragile, racked by her physical urges—totally unaware that, for him, this whole thing was little more than an act of revenge. To make her pay for how she had treated his brother and to salve his own conscience, if he was honest with himself, for his own contribution to his brother's reckless behaviour. She was unscrupulous, it was true, but she still wasn't well—and he couldn't use her like that.

'I think you'd better get dressed,' he advised, pushing himself up, away from her.

On his feet, he was already reinstating his clothes. 'I was right,' he said as she sat up, looking hurt and bewildered. 'This isn't a good idea.'

Abandoned as he closed the bedroom door behind him, not really sure of what she had done wrong, Sienna could only deduce, with a stinging slap to her pride, that it was her lack of sophistication and her failure to please him that had put him off.

Which was no more than she deserved, she reproached herself, for imagining she could make him like her—never mind allowing him to take such liberties with her body! She could only put it down to slight mental derangement caused by her very vulnerable state. She knew what he thought about her and it wasn't very complimentary! And even if her opinion of him had changed considerably since yesterday, it didn't mean that his had softened in any way towards her. It clearly hadn't! she realised shamefully. She would just have to be careful never to let him catch her off-guard again.

Daisy was helping one of the gardeners with his planting, Sienna noticed when, still embarrassed by the intimacies she had allowed herself to share with Conan, she came down into the garden a little later.

Ascertaining that the man didn't mind, and that Daisy wasn't hindering his work, she looked gingerly about her to see if Conan was around. He wasn't, but surprisingly she found Avril in her usual floppy hat, pruning a bright yellow shrub that bordered the terrace.

Intending merely to enquire how she was, and to

thank her for the flowers she'd sent up to her room the previous day, she was even more surprised when, after she'd done that, the woman gestured her towards a shady bower clothed with climbing burgundy roses which cleverly screened a smoky glass-topped wicker table and two matching chairs. There was a large jug of iced orange juice on the table.

'I understand you had a bit of an accident last night?' the woman remarked, filling two tall glasses from the jug and handing one to Sienna.

So Avril knew about that, Sienna realised, her colour rising, wondering who had told Conan's mother—Conan or Claudette?—and also whether Avril knew that her younger son's widow had spent the night and half the morning in her elder son's bed!

'Yes, I'm sorry about the vase,' she said contritely, deciding to bluff her way through it. 'Was it valuable?'

'Not particularly. It was a gift from my late husband when we became engaged.'

'Oh, gosh! I'm sorry,' Sienna repeated, feeling awful.

Avril, though, was waving her apologies aside. 'Don't be. It wasn't one of my favourites. Besides, I'm surprised it survived this long.'

The woman was being surprisingly blasé, Sienna thought, over losing something that must have meant a great deal to her. She wondered if the other woman was putting on a brave face to spare her discomfort.

'I know I can't replace its sentimental value, but would you at least let me buy you another?' Sienna offered, still feeling dreadful about it.

'Don't be silly,' Avril scolded lightly. 'As you said, it's irreplaceable. So don't try.'

Feeling a little chastened, Sienna was surprised when a sun-speckled hand covered hers where it was resting on the table. 'Besides, if I want another Conan will buy me one.' There was a strangely wistful note in the woman's voice as she added, with an almost rueful smile, 'He usually supplies me with everything I need.'

Sienna felt her cheeks burning again just at the mention of Conan's name, as sensual images of what had transpired in his room earlier caused her blood to race.

'He's a good son.'

An eyebrow cocked curiously under the floppy hat. Had Avril picked up on the rather breathless way she'd said that? Sienna wondered, dismayed, and was sure of it when the woman responded by advising, 'Don't imagine that you can get close to him, Sienna. Many women have tried—women who, if you don't mind me saying so, were a lot more steel-edged and sophisticated than you are. They've all been disappointed.'

'Perhaps he just hasn't found the right woman yet,' she returned, without thinking, and then wondered why she'd said it. Just as Avril must be wondering, she thought, when she saw that eyebrow climb even higher under the floppy hat. 'Don't worry. You've got no reason to fear that I'm likely to be taking another of your sons away from you,' she appeased, forcibly reiterating what she had promised Avril that evening Conan had come in and surprised them. And though she hadn't intended to sound bitter, she knew she did.

'Oh, I lost Conan a long time ago,' the woman startled her by saying. 'I think that's why I couldn't accept you as easily as I should have, Sienna. I couldn't bear the realisation I was losing my other son as well.'

Which she had—in the end. So pointlessly and so finally, Sienna thought, feeling for Niall's mother and yet amazed by her admission. She decided against reminding her that it was only her unfriendly attitude towards her younger son's new wife that had stopped her from gaining a daughter.

'What do you mean you lost him?' she pressed,

needing to know what Avril had meant by that remark about losing Conan. 'How? I thought that you and he were—'

'Were what? Close?' A strained little laugh infiltrated the still scented air, and the face across the table was suddenly ravaged by some private emotion. 'We put on a united front,' she informed Sienna almost bitterly. 'This family's always been very good at that.' She lifted the glass in her hand and took a long draught of her orange juice. There was a small round patch of condensation on the table where the glass had stood. When she put it down, her face was turned away, as though she was studying the deeply perfumed roses interlaced with the latticework of the bower. 'I let him down, Sienna. And it's something for which I shall reproach myself for the rest of my life.'

'Let him down?' she prompted, puzzled. 'How?'

The woman gave her head a couple of quick shakes, as though she was trying to clear it of a subject that was too personal or too painful for her to talk about.

'You must have done something right,' Sienna assured her with a smile. 'Or he wouldn't have turned out quite as confident and successful and level-headed and…dependable as he is today.'

Another knowing look was angled in her direction. 'Well…he certainly seems to have scored a hit with you.'

She hadn't realised how much she had been eulogising and, blushing furiously, keen to distract Avril from suspecting how Conan affected her, she uttered without thinking, 'Where did he get those scars?'

'Scars?' Beneath the floppy hat both eyebrows lifted in questioning surprise.

So Avril hadn't known how intimate they had been. But she did now!

Sienna realised. Because how else would her daughter-in-law have known about those old wounds, she guessed Avril must be thinking, if she hadn't seen Conan totally naked?

'Didn't he tell you?' the woman enquired, somewhat cagily.

'Only that they were caused by a dog,' Sienna informed her, deciding to brazen it out. 'And he said something about being somewhere he shouldn't have been.'

'Which was in the grounds of a private business premises which had been securely locked for the night.'

'Conan?' Sienna queried, bemused. What was Avril saying? That he had been a tearaway? Was that what the woman had meant by losing him?

'Not quite what you're thinking,' Avril said knowingly, aware of the path Sienna's thoughts had taken. 'He went in after Niall—and after he had already warned him what would happen if he went over that fence. But Niall was born with a need always to do what was reckless and dangerous and downright inadvisable...'

Which was how he had had that accident, Sienna thought, guessing from that crack in his mother's voice that she was thinking the same thing.

'He wouldn't listen,' Avril was continuing. 'He was only just twelve years old to Conan's sixteen at the time, but he *had* to test his brother's authority. Had—as it turned out—to put his brother's life on the line. Because of course when Conan heard the rumpus, with the dogs barking and Niall shrieking, he just went over that fence into those grounds without a thought for his own safety. Niall was pinned down by one of the dogs, but the other one...'

She couldn't go on. She didn't have to. Sienna could visualise it all too clearly, even without seeing the anguish scoring the pale, fragile lines of her mother-in-law's face.

No wonder he'd seemed so...tense, she thought, her heart aching for him, when Shadow had jumped up at him that night he'd first called at her house. It also explained why he'd been so angry on that other occasion when Jodie had said she'd left Daisy in the garden with Shadow.

'He was in hospital for a couple of days,' Avril went on, her voice strung with the same anguish as she continued. 'And both boys were let off with a warning as there were no previous offences and my husband was such an upstanding member of the community.'

'But Conan was all right,' Sienna stressed, realising the distress that reliving the incident was causing his mother. 'It could have been far, far worse.'

'Oh, yes. He was all right,' Avril supplied with an undertone of acidity. Or was it remorse? Sienna thought, wondering why. 'And things would have stayed all right if my husband hadn't been determined to get to the bottom of it. He wasn't exactly a man known for his restraint. Niall was too frightened to tell him the truth, and it was beyond Conan's ethics to drop his brother into the front line of his father's anger. You see, Sienna, my husband could be a very intimidating man. So he made Conan pay—or tried to. He'd always made him pay for everything—except Conan was big enough and strong enough by then not to take it any more. He left the following spring and I didn't see him again for years, until after my husband died. As I'm sure you already know, Conan wasn't his son. He was the result of a one-night affair I had with a young pilot while I was on holiday in the Channel Islands. I was carefree, irresponsible and crazy. Crazily in love for those few hours, or so I convinced myself. I didn't even know his last name.

'Conan and I were close for those first few years. But then after I married Niall's father and my younger son came along the favouritism started, with Conan never being able to do anything right in his stepfather's eyes. He was so bitterly jealous of Conan—always goading him. Belittling him. I suspect it was my fault for loving Conan so much. He hasn't said as much, but I know he blames me for allowing it to happen. After all, I could have done something about it. Got him away from his stepfather. Divorced him. But in spite of all that I suppose I still loved him. And anyway, I was afraid that if I did it would be my word against his and he'd get custody of Niall—and that was more than I could bear to contemplate. So you see, Sienna, I sacrificed Conan's welfare for the sake of his brother and I shan't blame him if he never forgives me. Because I shall never, ever forgive myself for that.'

Stunned, Sienna regarded Conan's mother, her

own features almost as harrowed. Avril hadn't meant to spill it out, she decided, and yet when all the pent-up anguish of a lifetime had started pouring out of her she hadn't been able to stop.

'Perhaps it's time to forgive yourself,' she suggested, doing as Avril had done earlier and slipping a hand over hers. 'I'm sure he doesn't think badly of you,' she murmured, her heart nevertheless going out to him. 'Otherwise he wouldn't worry about you quite as much as I know he does.'

'You know…you really are quite a perceptive and sensitive little thing.'

A rare warmth broke through the anguish scoring Avril's strained features. Like a chink in a wall letting the sunlight in, Sienna thought, giving her an insight into how beautiful the woman must once had been.

'I didn't ever dream that the little girl I resented would have the ability to make me open my heart to her—let alone try to make me feel better. And I *am* feeling a little better—both mentally and, I'm pleased to say, physically, too, over the past couple of days,' she expressed. 'Which is why I really don't want to see you get hurt. I know you have some sort of crush on Conan—there's no use denying it,' she interjected with a wry smile as Sienna made to try. 'Good heavens! I'm not altogether surprised—I've seen the effect he's had on women over the years. But I don't want to see you winding up unhappy over losing another of my sons, and I think you'd be on a collision course with disaster if you set your compass on Conan. He's too hard-bitten for you, Sienna. Apart from which, I think it's only fair to tell you that if you're living in the hope of his returning any feeling you think you might have for him, there's already one young woman of his acquaintance who considers herself first in the queue.'

She meant Petra Flax. Sienna didn't even need to ask. Not that she wanted to seem as though she was that interested, because she wasn't—was she? she assured herself. She'd made a big enough mistake in tying herself down the first time. She didn't have any plans for making the same mistake again any time soon.

'Good luck to her,' she murmured casually, excusing herself to go and check on Daisy, and deciding as she wound her way back through the scented garden that it was only because she'd been unwell that she felt so low.

CHAPTER EIGHT

CONAN woke up in bed, trembling and sweating. At first he thought he had caught Sienna's virus, until he realised it was only the effects of his dream.

Bringing her here had revived too many memories, he thought angrily. Of how much he had wanted her and how much he had beaten himself up over it, which in turn had reminded him of Niall, and of the darker past.

Getting up, he shrugged into his robe. The scent of her still clung to the garment from her wearing it two days ago, and, chastising himself for the way his body responded to it, he fastened the belt and went quietly downstairs without bothering to turn on a light.

Her shyness had surprised him. So had his own scruples. She had been ready for him, and yet he'd denied her. Denied himself, he thought with an ironic twist to his mouth and that familiar ache whenever he thought about her stirring in his loins. But why?

A prickly feeling down his spine lifted the hairs at the nape of his neck.

Feeling that he wasn't alone, he glanced round, his brows drawing together as he realised why. The dog had obviously padded down after him, and was standing in the doorway watching him.

A vision flashed through his brain. A set of bared white teeth. A huge snarling snout. And a black silhouette springing up out of the darkness. He felt the clamp of angry jaws, and the warm, bruising power of its body, then the pain and the fear. Fear such as he had never known before or since.

Clammy-skinned, he shook off the unwanted emotion in the way he had shaken off his dreams. 'You show up everywhere you're not wanted, don't you?' he drawled over his shoulder, opening the fridge.

The hiss of the cap being twisted off the bottle of mineral water he'd taken out was a soothing normality before he sat down with it on the cushioned cane sofa that ran along one wall, welcoming the burn of the chilled water as it slid down his throat.

Bringing her here wasn't doing much for his peace of mind or his self-respect, he thought self-deprecatingly. Because heaven only knew the feelings she generated in him weren't feelings he would normally have been too proud of. But then what man *would* be proud of harbouring such animosity towards his brother's widow, while wanting to do the most intimate things to her that his mind could dream up?

The dog padded over to him, unaware of his rising tension.

Or perhaps it was, he thought. Every cell in his body was shooting onto instinctive alert as the dog came much too close—close enough to lay a big hairy head on his bare knee.

Hesitantly he reached out, and with long tentative fingers ruffled the fur on the surprisingly gentle head. It felt warm, offering him a comfort he'd never expected to find.

'We're two of a kind, aren't we?' he murmured thickly, relaxing, experiencing for the first time a strange affinity with the animal. Didn't he come from the same ball-park as this four-legged freak? A nobody from nowhere? At least that was what his stepfather had tried to convince him he was. Of uncertain pedigree. With half his lineage unknown. The only difference was that this poor creature had been rescued, while there had been no one and nothing to rescue him.

Memories rose like dark demons, clouding his eyes and slashing harsh lines across his face, but forcefully he shook them away.

It was the past that had made him what he was. Driven. Motivated. A success in the eyes of the world. Sometimes it took all that he was made of to remind himself of that.

Hearing a sound, he glanced up, his wits sharper even than Shadow's.

Or perhaps the dog was just wallowing in stringing out this unexpected affection from him, he thought wryly, as its head swivelled round a second after he'd spotted Sienna standing in the doorway.

'Am I interrupting something personal?' she whispered, sounding surprised as well as amused. 'Do the two of you want to be left alone?'

She was wearing a short cotton polka dot robe, fastened loosely over a matching nightdress which showed off the soft movement of her breasts as she came in.

'What is it with the pair of you?' The barest smile touched his lips, and a toss of his chin indicated both her and Shadow, who had left him for this new and more appreciated visitor, his long tail waving gently. 'Can't you leave a man to his own devices without needing to invade his privacy?'

'I heard a sound. I looked in to see if Daisy was all right and noticed that Shadow was gone. I just came down to see where he was, but if that's how you feel…'

'Stay where you are.'

The deep, low command brought her head up, pulling her round as she was about to make her exit.

'But I thought you said…'

'Your sex doesn't have the monopoly on meaning the opposite of what you say,' he advised, with something tugging at the corners of his stupendous mouth.

'On what men *believe* is the opposite of what we say?' she was quick to amend firmly. 'There's a difference.'

'As I'm well aware.'

Which he would be, she thought. Intuition alone assured her that, regardless of his opinion of her, Conan Ryder was a man who would respect women just as surely as he knew how to pleasure them. The thought of what had transpired in his bed made her blood pulse quickly through her veins, so that it was a little breathlessly that she said, 'Are you asking me to stay?'

'Be my guest.'

She didn't take up his invitation to join him on the cane sofa. Sharing that particular seat would heighten her already screaming responses and make her more vulnerable to his devastating masculinity, and she wasn't sure she could handle the outcome of that, no matter how much she wanted it.

Instead she propped herself against the huge wooden table that stood in the middle of the room, her hands splayed out behind her.

'Do you want something to drink?' He gestured towards the fridge with the bottle he was drinking from.

Sienna shook her head, her hair a dark cap in the subdued light from the under-cupboard wall fittings which were all Conan had switched on. Her mouth felt dry, she realised, but it wasn't water that her foolish body craved.

Conan's mouth tugged carelessly on one side before his own dark head dropped back against the chintzy cushions of the sofa, the thick sweep of his lashes pressing down over the inscrutable gold of his eyes.

He looked hot and unusually tired, Sienna thought, glimpsing—surprisingly—a rare vulnerability behind that self-contained façade he presented to the world.

He was everything a woman could want, she realised, secretly studying him, her hungry eyes taking in the strong, lean bone structure that assured he would always stand out in a crowd, even without that added air of authority he exuded, or the head-turning lines of a physique that was primed to peak condition.

His reflexes were quick as a cobra's which, with that daunting ruthlessness, must have long ago earmarked him as a leader. Yet sensing vulnerability, remembering what Avril had told her, Sienna felt her heart swell with an emotion she didn't want to question too closely, and murmured in a voice made husky from that emotion, 'What's wrong?'

Her trembling question parted his lashes, bringing his unsettling gaze with unwavering directness to hers.

'Does something have to be wrong?' His smile, as he sat upright, said there wasn't. But there was, she thought, sensing it in every taut muscle of his powerful body. 'Do you know me so well that you think you can detect every nuance in my mood and character?'

'I don't think any woman could ever know you that well, Conan.'

His mouth moved contemplatively. 'You think I'm that deep?'

'I know you are.'

'And do you consider yourself qualified to plumb the depths?'

'I wasn't aware qualifications were required even if I thought of myself as a contender,' she breathed, wondering where this conversation had come from. 'Which I'm not.'

'And now I've upset you.'

'No, you haven't,' she said quickly, catching the sound of Shadow's claws on the quarry tiles as he trotted out of the kitchen, almost certainly to the comfort of Daisy's bed.

'Haven't I?' With his dark head cocked, Conan's gaze was far too shrewd, much, much too probing.

'It takes a lot more than that to upset me, Conan.'

There was a crack in her voice, he noted, that he couldn't quite account for. Contention, maybe, but if it wasn't then something was certainly affecting her.

She was outspoken, which he liked. In fact he found it distinctly refreshing. Most women he had known who were contenders for his bed had usually started out by agreeing with everything he liked, did and said—not challenging him at every given opportunity like this little madam. And yet that husky quality to her voice was doing untold things to his libido.

She was leaning back, supporting herself against the table, the action causing her robe to part and pushing up her beautiful breasts so that their soft upper swell was clearly visible to him above the simple nightdress.

He wanted her, he realised at that moment, swallowing a mouthful of cold water to try and temper his urges, more than he had wanted any woman in his life. Wanted her even as she was looking at him as doe-eyed as an innocent, and with that sort of anguished groove between her velvety eyebrows.

'Why are you looking at me like that?' he found himself asking her.

Sienna's breath seemed to shiver through her lungs, lifting her far too tender breasts to that hot masculine gaze.

Her lips parted as she dragged in air, hesitating, unintentionally provocative as she sought the courage to tell him, say the things she wanted—needed—to say.

'I only—' She swallowed, put off by that invisible barrier she could feel as tangibly as a shield of iron between them—a barrier she had always sensed Conan had deliberately erected between himself and the rest of the world. Like a dark and vigilant observer, aloof and protected by his own impregnable wall of immunity. 'Avril told me what happened when you got attacked by that dog. And about your father. I mean…' her throat worked nervously again '…your stepfather. What went on.'

Anger, like a dart of green lightning, flashed momentarily in his eyes, before his lashes came down, sweeping it away, leaving only a grim emotion that stretched his tanned skin taut across his angular features.

'What did she tell you? That he brutalised me mentally and physically?' He unfolded his long length from the padded seat and came towards her, the plastic bottle still in his hand. 'That he gave me the shelter of his home and the respectability of his name and made me pay for both of them through and through?' His bitterness was so palpable it dragged across her skin like the serrated edge of a knife.

'I'm sorry.' It sounded trite and utterly ineffectual against the depth of emotion that welled up for him from some hidden place deep inside her—such a breath-catching emotion that it was a moment before she could continue. 'She feels she let you down in not leaving him. That she put up with the way he treated you out of fear of losing your brother. She's tortured by it, Conan.'

'Is she?' he exhaled through the grinding tension of his jaw. 'And what else did she tell you? That he brutalised her too? That he made her pay for every occasion when she took my side against his? A respected barrister. A man at the cutting edge of his profession. A so-called "pillar of society."' Derision coloured his tone, his mouth contorting in distaste. 'He made her pay and never stopped making her pay until I was old enough to take matters into my own hands and knocked him flat.'

Sienna could feel the colour draining out of her cheeks, unable to imagine a man like Conan ever being driven into losing his cool like that.

'I see that she didn't,' he said grimly, assessing the shock and disbelief on her small blanched face. 'She wouldn't leave him, so in the end I had to. If I hadn't, I think I might have killed him.' He was so close now that she could feel the anger emanating from him as he put the bottle down on the table beside her. 'Life was intolerable for us all until I did. My mother was suffering and being made to pay because of me, and Niall was just caught in the middle.' He remembered his brother's tears and his frightened trembling, his sobbed and heartfelt promises—always sincerely meant after he had been too weak to admit to some wrongdoing— that he would never get him into trouble again. 'After I'd left my stepfather got what he wanted. His wife and his own son to himself, and from what I gather peace reigned from then on in the household. It seemed I was the source of all my stepfather's problems. The font from which all his jealousy sprang.'

The horror of all he had said sent a chill

through Sienna, causing her to shudder physically. Straightening up, she automatically put her hand out to him, her slender, pink-tipped fingers shaping the taut outline of one hard masculine cheek.

'I'm sorry. I'm so, so sorry.' Her feeling for him almost choked her, her words erupting from her on the tide of emotion that was flooding every fibre of her being.

His mouth lifted at one corner: a half smile—superficial, ironic, self-mocking.

'Is that why you were looking at me the way you were looking at me just now? Out of pity?' he challenged thickly. It struck him then that this was the first and only time he had ever bared his soul to anyone. It left him feeling uncomfortably exposed and vulnerable.

'I think pity would be wasted on you, Conan,' she said with unerring frankness. 'As well as being an insult,' she added tremulously, as she brought both hands into play to caress the soft towelling sheathing his broad shoulders, marvelling at how all that strength and latent power beneath her fingers could contain such a well of hidden anguish.

His smile this time was warm and unmistakably sensual, and Sienna's heart leaped as he caught her hand, turning it over to press his lips to the sensitive area of her wrist, allowing his teeth to graze gently along the inside of her arm. 'Clever answer,' he murmured silkily.

Riveted by his action, by his scent and his warmth and the breath-catching reality of his closeness, with a sensuous little shudder, she uttered, 'I'm not trying to be clever, Conan.'

His head lifted, his eyes meeting and locking with hers.

'No,' he breathed deeply in acceptance, and with his arm snaking around her waist very gently he drew her towards him.

She couldn't drag her eyes from his—not until his face went out of focus. Then she slid her arms around him, gasping into his mouth at the coldness of his right hand on her bare skin just above the back of her nightdress, from where he had been holding the chilled bottle.

'I'm sorry,' he murmured, scarcely lifting his mouth from hers, and yet she could still detect the warm concern in his voice.

'It's all right.' She sighed against the day's growth of stubble beneath his lower lip, because nothing he did to her would ever be anything but all right. She didn't know how she knew that, but she did.

His lips—like his arms—for all their strength were infinitely tender. So much so that she felt a well of emotion pressing against her chest. Because what she needed most of all right now was tenderness. Just as *he* did, she realised, with both hands coming up to cup his face, her tongue probing and exploring, melding with his as, with one arm supporting her back, he tipped her gently backwards until he was lying over her on the table.

'Oh, Conan…' Above the quiet hum of the fridge her voice was like a woodland nymph's—no more than a sigh lost on a transient breeze.

She wanted this, she realised now. Had wanted it from the moment he had taken her in his arms on the dance floor at that company dinner—refusing to acknowledge it, despising herself for even imagining what it could be like…

'Hush, hush.' He pacified her between the whisper of kisses over her face and throat, his tenderness so arousing that when he took her lips again, deepening the kiss with intensifying eroticism, she groaned her need into his mouth.

'Not now. Not yet,' he murmured with a teasing warmth in his voice, although she could tell from the way his breath shuddered through him that he was having difficulty keeping control. 'You belong in my bed, Sienna. Not here, like some cheap grabbed thrill with the boot boy—even if it is tempting to throw caution to the winds and savour the added thrill of the risk of being found out.'

How did he know that she felt like that? That she didn't care any more about who saw them? That she almost welcomed the idea of being discovered so that the whole wide world would know that this man was her lover?

And if she felt like that, then surely it must mean...

That she loved him?

But how could she? she wondered, shocked, when she had promised herself faithfully that she would stay immune. And not just with him, but with any man?

With her mouth welded to his, she sighed her despair against their mingled breath before he lifted her up, and with such little effort that she might have been weightless, carried her almost soundlessly up the marble stairs.

Did he know? He could tell what she was feeling—thinking—couldn't he? So how could she hide whatever this feeling was when her body was betraying her with its desperate need to be closer to him, craving his loving and his attention? When it always would, she thought hopelessly, just at a smile from him or a simple word...

His room was dimly lit, from where a gap in the curtains allowed the beams of a nearly full moon to creep through. But its shapes were familiar to her like the familiar surroundings of someone visually impaired.

Which she was, wasn't she? she thought with an abandoned excitement. Because they said love was blind, and she had to be blind if she could ignore the warnings of the person who knew him better than anyone about getting so intimately involved with him, if she wanted to scream out to the world that he was her lover as she had wanted to do downstairs.

He moved as stealthily as a panther across the room with her to the enormous bed, and she detected a hint of sensual amusement as he set her down on the cool sheet and said in a voice thickened from the strength of his desire for her, 'This is getting to be a habit.'

'Yes…' Her breathing was as laboured as his, her murmur a simple acquiescence of all they were going to do and what they were about to become, of the changing of the balance of their relationship for good.

And how foolish was that? An inner little voice tried breaking through her sensual lethargy to goad her, but she was already too far beyond the bounds of reason to listen.

Blotting out everything but the stimulating impulses that were driving her, she was reaching for him as he slid in beside her, discovering with a spiralling excitement from the warmth of his hair-roughened skin that he had already discarded his robe.

'Love me,' she murmured, pulling him down to her, offering her eager body to him with an abandonment which she knew now she had never offered his brother. Not with this cauldron of mutual need and desire, she thought.

And then Conan's lips and hands and the whole electrifying weight of his body numbed her to everything else but the galvanising sensations that were driving her mindless for him. Although the way he slowed the pace in measured, leisurely adoration of her body kept her on fire until she thought she would implode if he didn't grant her the release and fulfilment she craved.

When it finally came it had her gasping above the shuddering groans that accompanied his own burning orgasm, an all-consuming mutual inferno of pleasure that lasted and lasted and lasted.

It was such a profoundly moving experience that as the final contractions throbbed out of her Sienna's emotions welled up in scalding tears, which gave way to uncontrolled sobs that shook her slender body.

Held against his shoulder, she let it all out, a torrent of hot, unleashed emotion that she couldn't have held back if her life had depended upon it.

'I'm sorry. I'm so sorry.' Ashamed, she tried to get up, but the gentle touch of his fingers pressed her back as he raised himself up sufficiently so that he could look at her.

'What is it? What's wrong?' he enquired, sounding deeply concerned.

Sienna shook her head, unable to answer. How could you tell a man who didn't particularly like you—let alone respect you—that making love with him had been the best experience of her twenty-five years? Ever. How could you do that unless you also told him that you thought you were falling in love with him? And only a fool would do that after all she had been through.

Sniffing back emotion, she shook her head again, trying to regain control, some degree of dignity.

'Do you always cry like this after you make love?' He sounded gently amused, yet surprised too.

'Don't all women?' she parried, grasping the clean, folded white handkerchief he'd just reached over and taken out of the drawer of his bedside cabinet.

'No.'

She smiled weakly, blowing her nose. 'Then it must be the effect you have on me.'

'Clearly,' he agreed, with a cocked smile. His thick winged brows were drawing together in puzzled bewilderment. What was she saying? That she hadn't been like this with any of the other men she'd known? Before he knew it, he was asking, 'What happened between you and my brother?'

Of course. He still believed she'd had a lover.

She didn't answer at first. How could she, she thought, when there were some things that were far too personal?

Striving to sit up, she was relieved when he permitted it this time.

'We were having problems,' she admitted, looking down at the handkerchief she was twisting in her hands. 'We always seemed to be arguing in the end.'

'What about?' he pressed.

'I don't know.' She gave a little shrug. 'Everything. Money. Daisy. His drinking.'

I'm sorry. I'm so, so sorry...

The regrets of that other time echoed down the years, but mentally she shook them away.

'Sienna?'

Lying on his side now, supported by his elbow, he could see the tension in her slender back—the way she was holding herself rigid as though she was fighting an inner battle with herself. One that hurt—like hell.

He placed a hand on her shoulder, his touch gentle but firm, and compliantly she allowed him to draw her back into the warm circle of his arms.

'His job. Being a father. His debts. I think it was all too much for him,' she murmured, her voice sounding far away. 'And he was always working so hard. Driving himself...' *To try and compete with you,* she added mentally, but didn't say it. 'We even stopped making love. I thought it was all my fault. Because I was tired looking after Daisy. I thought maybe motherhood had made me unattractive...'

Conan laughed softly, his eyes incredulous. 'Are you kidding? Your pregnancy, Sienna, made you blossom—and, believe me, it lasted.' He didn't tell her that there had been times when he'd found himself thoroughly envying his brother. Aside from all those other occasions, he thought, when he'd been a child, desperate for his stepfather's approval. For one ounce of the praise and affection his brother had taken as his birthright. 'I wanted you, Sienna.'

His comments had made her blush, he noticed, stroking her damp cheek, watching colour infuse the delicate skin. 'And it was mutual, wasn't it?' he prompted, thinking how her unexpected disclosure might go some way to explaining why she had taken a lover, even if it didn't excuse it. And why he had picked up on those pheromones she'd given off whenever she was alone in his company, but particularly at that dinner-dance that night. But was it because of *him?* Or had her lack of sex with Niall made her that desperate for a man? Any man? he wondered, finding the thought less than flattering, though he knew he had no right even thinking that way about the woman who'd been married to his brother. 'Tell me the truth.' For all his ethics about what was right and wrong, it was suddenly imperative that he should know.

'You overwhelmed me, that's all,' she dissembled, sitting up again. Because there was being straight with him, and there was being downright stupid. There was no way she was going to tell him exactly how she had felt when he had taken her in his arms that night because she had only just realised it herself. And because… Well, because she just couldn't, that was all. 'I know you don't want to accept it,' she tagged on, her blue gaze coming level with his, 'but I never cheated on your brother.'

His eyelids came down, concealing what he was thinking, his chest lifting and falling heavily.

Did he believe her? she wondered, aching for

him to tell her so and realising now that she *had* to make him understand.

'Tim's mother and my dad were some sort of distant cousins. They were like family, and we all used to go on holiday together. When Tim's parents moved to Spain he was only seventeen, and he wanted to stay in England, so Mum and Dad let him move in with us. We used to go clubbing together, or to the cinema if one of us was at a loose end. He was part of the gang I kicked around with.' Her childhood playmate. The son of the couple she'd always called Aunt and Uncle. And, after he'd moved in, the big brother she'd never had. 'When Mum and Dad decided to move to Spain too, and I got my flat, they asked him if he'd keep an eye on me. There was never anything romantic between us,' she stressed, needing to convince him.

Because for Timothy Leicester there had never been anyone but Angie Thompson. Angie who had given him the runaround at school and at college, until just before she went away to university when she'd realised he was the nicest thing walking on two legs.

'I looked on him as a brother, and his girlfriend was like a sister to me until she went off to Brazil to save the rainforest. When you turned up at Tim's place that morning to tell me what had happened to Niall—I know how it must have looked, but you wouldn't listen to the things I've just told you— then or afterwards—when I tried to explain.' Because all he had seen in that one bedroom flat was a rumpled double bed, and belongings lying around that were exclusively masculine. And he had already been persuaded of her guilt, she remembered, by the people who had had her investigated. 'Angie was already in Brazil, and I knew Tim was planning to join her, but I—' She broke off, her breath coming shallowly, suddenly finding it impossible to articulate the words that would vindicate her. 'I just wanted to see him before he went,' she said instead.

'When I turned up with Daisy and decided to stay the night he gave up the bedroom and slept on the sofa. I tidied it up after he'd left for work,' she went on. So there had been nothing but her futile attempt—already muddled by the shock of learning about Niall—to convince his brother that he hadn't just stepped into an illicit love-nest. 'I was too upset to string two sentences together.' So numbed by what had happened and by everything that had driven her to Tim's that weekend that she hadn't even been able to cry. So Conan had decided she didn't care. 'I was also scared stiff of you,' she admitted, with a rather sheepish smile. 'As I said, you overwhelmed me.'

He inclined his head ever so slightly, in the briefest of acknowledgements. But of what? she wondered piercingly. That she was telling the truth? Was that what had brought his incredible lashes down over his eyes and made his breath seem to shiver through him? Or was it just relief in deciding at last that he wasn't sleeping with the enemy?

'And what about now, Sienna?' he exhaled, disappointing her because he didn't actually say he believed her. Although she hadn't actually told him everything, had she? she admitted to herself, already starting to tingle from the sensuality with which he pressed, 'Do I overwhelm you *now?*'

That sexiness of his voice and the way he was looking at her with such a febrile glitter in his eyes made her pulses start to throb, sending a resurgence of hot desire licking along her veins.

'No, you've just made me realise that I've got you exactly where I want you,' she murmured provocatively, pushing him back so that she could admire the flawed perfection of his amazing body.

Sensuously then, and very slowly, she anointed him with kisses, her tongue marking a path along the line of dark hair that ran from his chest, down over his waist to his tight, lean abdomen, straying only to pay particular attention to those angry slashes that spoke so vividly of his character, and were testimony to the sort of man he was.

A brave and honourable one, she thought, otherwise he wouldn't have shown such a strong sense of responsibility towards his weaker and reckless younger brother. And not just with those dogs, but in everything, she decided, her feeling for him ballooning inside her until it almost hurt keeping it to herself.

But she had to, she resolved grittily, guessing that he probably wouldn't welcome what he might think was a love-struck, clingy female in his bed any more than she intended to allow herself to become one. She understood now though why he'd threatened to take Daisy from her in the past, and why he'd vetoed the thought of any other man stepping into her life, and subsequently into Daisy's, when he'd had a stepfather as cold and brutal as he'd had.

Wanting to heal him more than she could ever express in words, and touching him in the most intimate place, she watched with darkened eyes as his face was scored almost with pain and his jaw clamped tightly as he groaned his need of her.

Made bold by his response, and the realisation of her strong yet reluctant love for him, she pleasured him then in the way she had wanted to please him since that first morning she'd woken up in his bed, driving him wild for her until he finally lost control and surrendered to the power of her femininity.

CHAPTER NINE

THE days that followed were halcyon ones for Sienna. She was living in a fragile bubble of happiness, she realised, which, like all bubbles, was by its very nature designed not to last.

Foolishly, though—and she knew she was being foolish—she allowed herself to enjoy the ecstatic feeling that she was floating on a cloud, buoyed up by Conan's insatiable need of her and hers for him, and kept there by the all-consuming fire of their lovemaking.

He could be excitingly passionate, she was discovering, when they had been made to wait to satisfy their intensifying and increasing appetite for each other because of the presence of Daisy and Avril, or simply because of the pressing demands of Conan's work. Unable to wait another second to satisfy their screaming hunger for each other, content that Daisy was safely preoccupied with Claudette or his mother, they would slink away like guilty lovers to some quiet area of his private beach, or out to the yacht he kept in the bay. There he would make hard and urgent love to her—just as her body demanded it—without any waiting or prolonged foreplay, driving her crazy with the knowledge that he wanted her with every breath of the passion with which she wanted him, and with shattering orgasms that left them both slick with sweat and gasping at the driving urgency with which he had taken her.

And then there were those other times, in the still of the night, between the sensuous satin of his sheets, when the rest of the world evaporated, when he would drive her delirious for him with a slow, calculated expertise that had her shuddering and sobbing for release. Then he would show her the true meaning of the phrase "sexual prowess" by bringing her to orgasm after multi-orgasm, before he finally allowed his amazing control to snap and lost himself in the hot and exquisite fulfilment her body offered.

Sienna would emerge the following morning, unable to conceal the glow in her cheeks, or the way her eyes were glittering like brilliant sapphires after a night of unparallelled rapture, her spirits high, her mood buoyant, while she ached for his lips and his hands on her body again with a crav-

ing that only making love with him could tempo-
rarily slake.

Conan, on the other hand, managed to appear remarkably unaffected—especially when they were
in the company of other people. While meeting
the pressing demands of his high-flying day-to-
day business, or joining her and Avril for a drink
on the terrace, or even inviting Sienna to accom-
pany him for a meal out with colleagues, he stayed
appropriately and yet amazingly aloof. Until he
glanced across at her from behind his mother's
chair or across a crowded table, and then the message in his eyes ignited a flame that would make
molten heat pool in her loins and keep her on fire
for him—sometimes for hours—until it culmi-
nated, as it always did on those occasions, in one
of the hottest and most basic of couplings that was
all the more thrilling for having been denied.

How they managed to keep their drastically al-
tered relationship from Daisy and Avril and everyone else in the house—with the exception perhaps
of Claudette—Sienna wasn't sure, except that
Conan had enough discretion for both of them. He
made no attempt to touch her if any of the others
were around, or only in the most casual of ways.
Like when helping her in and out of the dinghy
when they had a family day out on the yacht, or

giving her a hand up from the shingle where they had been playing with Daisy. And if Claudette alone wondered why there were two damp towels slung down on the base of his power shower, or two depressions on the pillows on his enormous bed, or even that the bronze leather surface of the desk she was polishing smelled of a sultry feminine perfume when the sun touched it, then she was obviously paid too highly—or, more probably, respected her employer too much—to disclose his very private affair.

Because it *was* an affair. Sienna wasn't so completely swept away not to realise that. After all, if she had been setting her sights on marriage— which she certainly wasn't, she assured herself— what could a girl like her ever hope to offer a man like him?

And when it ended, as it surely would, she accepted—when her euphoria was dampened by the thought of what she had got herself into, how awkward would it be remaining in touch with him—as she would have to, she realised, now that she had agreed to bring Daisy to see her father's family as regularly as her job would allow? It was something pointed out to her rather surprisingly, and not in so many words, by Avril one afternoon, when Sienna was helping her cut some blooms from the villa's magnificent white roses bushes.

'I hope you've thought about what you're doing, Sienna.' The caution was so sudden and yet so patently clear that Sienna looked up quickly from what she was doing and felt one of the vicious thorns prick her finger. 'I hope you have,' Avril emphasised. 'For all our sakes.'

Sienna turned away so that her mother-in-law wouldn't see the colour that washed up into her cheeks, sucking hard on her wound. The blood was bitter in her mouth—as bitter as the meaning behind Avril's warning.

'I won't do anything that will ever stop you seeing Daisy again,' Sienna promised, though a little shakily. Because wasn't she doing exactly that? she berated herself, noticing how much better Avril was looking than when Sienna had first come here, despite the anxiety that was still lining her somewhat gaunt features. The woman had more colour in her cheeks these days, and she was getting stronger by the day, taking on more adventurous tasks without getting breathless, which was thanks in part to the regime of gentle exercise that Sienna had set out for her, but mainly, she suspected, because Avril was enjoying a new sense of purpose in being able to focus on her little granddaughter.

Did she want to jeopardise all that through her own selfishness?

She was being a fool. She knew she was—had been telling herself since that night when she'd gone down to the kitchen looking for Shadow and found him with Conan, before she'd gone willingly into his arms and let him take her to bed. Hadn't she been advising herself day after day—when she managed to find some rational moment after he'd gone out and she could think with a clearer head—that she must call a halt to what was happening between them before it got out of hand? But she couldn't, she thought, ashamed of having to admit how weak she was where he was concerned. It was already out of hand.

Part of her had been half in love with him for a long time, she accepted now, although she hadn't realised it until that night. The night she'd discovered how unhappy his childhood had been, and she had opened up to him with everything that was caring and feminine in her when she'd realised just how cruel his stepfather had been and how isolated and undervalued he must have felt.

But if he hadn't then he might not have been so determined to make a success of himself, she thought, aching for the little boy who had felt like such an outcast, so underrated and alone. It was his childhood, most certainly, that must have contributed to that determination and to the steel-edged strength of his character, although he probably owed some of it to the young pilot who had fathered him, rather than Avril, who tended to let life ride roughshod over her, Sienna decided, thinking of the father who had never known Conan existed. But it had flawed him too, as his mother had already pointed out.

He didn't allow anyone close to him. So what right did she have to assume that one day he might—and that it would be her, she wondered dispiritedly, when she wasn't even ready to make another commitment herself? None, she told herself bluntly. Yet in spite of the talking to she kept giving herself, and the things Avril had just said, she couldn't help nursing the hope of a woman already lost to love, even while wondering how she could possibly have got herself into such a mess.

They spent the last afternoon of Sienna's time in the South of France making love in Conan's enormous bed, because Avril had taken Daisy to a children's fête in one of the neighbouring villages. Sienna had wanted to go with her daughter, thinking that the energetic four-year-old might prove too much of a handful for Conan's mother. But the little girl had protested, telling her very importantly that she was taking her grandmother all by herself—which Avril had been quick to second—and with Conan's chauffeur driving them to the fête, and Claudette going along to take the strain off the older woman, Sienna had reluctantly given in.

Now, tender in the aftermath of lovemaking, she was lounging naked on top of the duvet, supported by pillows and one arm behind her head, smiling as the bedroom door opened and Conan came in with a tray.

Having made love across lunchtime, and for the past couple of hours since, they were both famished, and Sienna had welcomed his suggestion of bringing something up from the kitchen. She could already smell the fresh crusty bread, and noticed, with her mouth watering, the white and gold wedges of the various cheeses he'd selected under a glass dome as he set the tray down on the table he'd already placed beside the bed. With his casual long-sleeved white shirt—tucked loosely into his pale chinos—gaping virtually to the waist, he looked the stuff of every woman's fantasy, and Sienna couldn't take her eyes off that tantalising swathe of bronzed, hair-roughened flesh while he was lifting the dome off the cheeses, any more than she could ignore the musky scent that emanated from him, and the scent of loving which still hung heavily in the room.

'Now.' He was tapping one of the cheese wedges with the curved end of the knife. 'What will you have?'

'You,' she breathed, her eyelids heavy from the sensual bonds which held her captive, finding it extremely erotic being naked when he was already dressed.

'You're decadent,' he murmured, his eyes glinting as he handed her one of the glasses of red wine he had brought up, his heated gaze roaming approvingly over her body.

'No. I'm not,' she countered, her excitement building just at the way he was looking at her. 'If I am, then it's your fault. Every little wicked thing I do, you're responsible for.' Taking a sip of the dark, full-bodied wine, she let the base of the tall glass rest on the dip between her tender, betraying breasts. 'Aren't you ashamed of yourself, Conan Ryder?'

He thought about what she'd said about his brother's interest in her waning, and wondered how any man could not want her. He could feel his urges rising again, but there were things that needed to be said.

'Don't do that.'

With her chin resting just above her chest, the glass tilted forward towards her, she was drawing her tongue suggestively around the rim of the glass while sweeping him a look of pure provocation.

'Why not?' Her smile teased, but she was all wide-eyed innocence as she did it again.

'Because if you don't stop it then I'm going to do something I'll be very ashamed of.'

'Like sending me back to bed with no dinner?' She giggled and slid down the bed, fully aware of the way what she was saying and doing was turning him on. 'Isn't that what you do with naughty girls who misbehave?'

'Sienna…'

Ignoring him, she wriggled further down the bed, with the base of the glass still pressed against the valley between her breasts, moving her hips so wantonly that the wine came precariously close to slopping out of the glass. 'Oops!'

'If you spill that…' Conan's voice warned of some delicious repercussions.

'Oh, dear!' She bit her lower lip in mock contrition. 'And it would be all over your nice clean sheets too.'

She gasped as the glass was suddenly whisked out of her hand.

'Sienna…we have to talk.'

His voice held all the gravity of something extremely serious. Like a doctor telling you there was no more room to hope. She heard it, but didn't want to acknowledge it—any more than she wanted to acknowledge that same seriousness mirrored in his eyes.

'We *are* talking,' she breathed tremulously, dark lashes pressed against the wells of her eyes so that she couldn't see that look of finality that was oh, so obvious in his eyes.

Tomorrow they would be flying back. What else was he going to tell her except that the holiday romance was over? No, not quite that—because it hadn't been a romance, had it? It had been the uncontrolled and desperate need of one man and one woman to do the most fundamental thing nature demanded of them. And if nature had had its way she would have been pregnant by him dozens of times over, she thought shamefully, except he had always been careful to take precautions.

As he was doing now, she realised, her senses leaping in wild anticipation, because her provocation had ultimately proved too much for him. She didn't need to open her eyes to recognise the sliding of the drawer in the bedside cabinet, and the familiar urgency of him ripping off his clothes.

It was quick and hot and hard, as once again she

obeyed nature's demands in her hopeless, insatiable craving for him, taking him into her with her legs clenched tightly around his taut hard waist, her fingers locking with his on either side of the pillow high above her head.

When it was over she collapsed beneath him, gasping from the shuddering contractions that had had her crying out with an emotion that had been almost too much to contain.

Now, as he came down on top of her, breathing as heavily as she was, he pressed his lips against the satin slope of her shoulder. After a few moments, in a voice roughened by passion, he advised thickly, 'Don't fall in love with me, Sienna.'

She had, she thought hectically, wondering if he had guessed—and wincing a little as he withdrew from her, as so much loving by him today had made her tender. He was after all experienced enough to recognise when a woman's responses were for real.

Why not? she wanted to demand, just for the sheer hell of it. As if she didn't know! Men like him didn't fall for girls like her. And if the beautiful and sophisticated women that he usually mixed with couldn't penetrate that hard veneer, what hope did a girl of her humble background have of succeeding?

Feigning nonchalance, she uttered, 'I wouldn't dream of it.' She even managed a painful little smile.

'I mean it,' Sienna.' He didn't even look at her as he got up from the bed. 'If you do, you'll only get hurt.'

He could feel her gaze following him as he paced away to the bathroom. He felt like a heel, he thought, but he couldn't lie to her. She had come to him that night when he had most needed her tender femininity and he had taken full advantage of it—over and over and over again.

As he dispensed with the condom and got himself back into some sort of order he thought back to four weeks ago, when he had first brought her here, and particularly to that antagonised scene with her in the pool.

It had been his intention to have a fling with her. Get his anger and his rampant desire for her out of his system. But it hadn't worked out as simply as that. The more he had of her, the more he wanted. And the more he took, surprisingly, the more it seemed she was prepared to give. It didn't help his conscience either to discover that, far from the lying little cheat he had always believed her to be, she appeared to be open and honest and entirely different from the girl he thought he had known.

There was nothing of the high-maintenance, possession-loving creature who had worn her designer clothes and jewellery like trophies three years ago. She dressed very simply, never seemed interested in any of the exclusive shops whenever she had the chance to browse around them. And whenever he had taken her and Daisy out for the day she'd always tried to insist on paying for her and his niece's share herself.

She was proud and dignified and unbelievably desirable. She was also making him question his own actions—and he didn't like that. Whatever she said, she was getting too involved with him—and *he,* he realised, like a fool, was in danger of allowing her to. He didn't want to hurt her, but neither did he want an emotional involvement with her. Even if he was being brutal, she had to know.

She was standing by the bed, pulling on her blue chequered shirt, when he came back into the bedroom wearing his robe. A glimpse of her bare breasts above the tight clinging jeans almost threw his determination to the winds.

'Why are you looking at me like that?' Her heavy-lidded eyes, he noticed, were dark and brooding.

'Like what?' she replied curtly, knotting the ends of her blouse just above her tiny waist.

'Like I'm the big bad wolf and you're Little Red Riding Hood.'

Perhaps I feel like Little Red Riding Hood, she thought silently. Chased. Caught. Pounced on. And ravenously devoured. It didn't help telling herself, no matter how bad she was feeling, that she had done her fair share of the devouring too.

'I'm sorry if I've disappointed you,' he was saying, 'because I'm not the soft-hearted sentimentalist you might have convinced yourself I was.'

The sun picked out snatches of red in her gleaming black hair as she brought her head up. 'You? Soft?' she said with a brittle little laugh. 'I think any woman—or man—would have to have their head read if they *ever* made the mistake of thinking you were soft.'

'Then what's eating you, Sienna?'

What's eating me, she thought, as she turned away and made a show of straightening the duvet, is that I love you. And even though I've never said it, you've as good as thrown it right back in my face.

'Nothing,' she murmured with a little shrug.

He couldn't see her face, only the taut movements of her back, and the way her jeans clung smoothly to the contours of her delightful little bottom as she tried to restore some order to the wreck of his love-scented bed.

'I've never lied to you, or given you any reason to expect the promise of a commitment,' he added tonelessly.

Thumping a pillow with unnecessary force, she said coolly, without glancing round, 'Have I ever asked you to?'

'No.' His eyes were darkly reflective as he stood there watching her. He'd messed this up good and proper, he thought, wanting to kick himself, knowing that he should have had this conversation with her weeks ago. 'And I'm not suggesting that we should end what we have.'

'Really?' She spun round, clutching another pillow tightly to her chest. 'What exactly *do* we have, Conan? Great sex?'

Something tugged at one corner of his mouth. 'You must admit it's pretty spectacular.'

Which was an understatement! she thought. They had been slightly more than obsessed with each other! At least in bed.

'So you're saying we go on as we are? With no strings attached?'

'If you're prepared to do that. I just want to be open with you, so you know from the start where you stand and you can make a decision. Just as long as you're aware that I'm not proposing to marry you.'

He couldn't have put it more plainly.

'So you want us to go on having great sex, so long as it's kept on a purely physical level?'

'You don't have to make it sound so cold-blooded,' he remarked, reaching for his glass of wine, which still remained untouched on the tray he'd brought up before they had been overtaken by the scorching inferno that continued to consume them with no sign of ever burning itself out.

'Don't I?' She tossed the plumped pillow back on the bed. 'So what did you expect? My loving gratitude? There aren't many women who wouldn't feel a little put out by such a high-handed, presumptuous statement. "Just as long as you're aware that I'm not proposing to marry you",' she mimicked, her hands clutching her elbows, punctuating each word with a little shake of her body. 'Well, for your information, Conan Ryder, who said I *wanted* to marry you? If you must know, I had enough of marriage and so-called connubial bliss with your wonderful brother. Why would I want to jump in feet first and tie myself down to *you?*'

Of course, he thought. She hadn't had a particularly good time of it with his brother. But she was saving face. He was sure of it. It made him want to take her in his arms and kiss away her painful indignation. But that was just sex driving him—he was sure of that too—and suddenly he felt angry with her for making him feel so guilty.

'Well, that told me, didn't it?' he said, putting down his glass and holding the feeling in check as he played along with what he strongly suspected was an all-out attempt to maintain her dignity. His annoyance though was being swiftly replaced by something fast approaching admiration. The re-action of most women he dismissed from his bed after an affair had run its course was usually one of tears or bitter recriminations. Sienna wasn't out-wardly displaying either. But then neither was he dismissing her from his bed. 'Which will just teach me to presume.'

'Yes, it will!' she underlined, wondering how—even when there was no future in it—when she hadn't even expected him to offer her one—she was going to find the strength to walk away from all that he was proposing. Which was little more than pure and simple ecstasy until such time as he called the shots by deciding he wanted to move on. 'But just for the record… If I were to agree to what you're suggesting—which I'm not,' she tagged on hastily, 'aren't you worried that I really might fall in love with you? Or worse.' With a feigned and shuddering little laugh she lifted her eyes to the ceiling. 'Heaven forbid! You might suddenly find yourself in love with *me!*'

'Stop it, Sienna.' Suddenly he couldn't bear what he could see clearly she was doing to herself. He didn't want pretence. He would have preferred tears, or at best a tirade of abuse from her. 'I don't intend allowing myself ever to fall in love with you. It won't happen. Do I make myself clear?'

'As crystal.' But her voice cracked as she said it. Why should it matter? she challenged herself. When another commitment with a man was something she had been determined to steer clear of? When falling for him didn't mean putting herself back into the kind of emotional tyranny she had known before? Still reeling from his statement, however, she uttered with all the dignity she could muster, 'Could you at least tell me what puts you in a position so enviously above the rest of us that you're able to set such store by your own immunity?'

She was too far removed from his social circle for him ever to fall in love with. He still didn't like her. She satisfied him in bed but was far too shallow to satisfy his intellectual needs. The possibilities rang through her brain and none of them were complimentary. Or perhaps it was simply that he was in love with Petra Flax.

He had been pulling on his clothes, and his shirt was now hanging loosely over his chinos as it had been before they had both been overcome by their escalating need for each other.

'I came from one fractured family,' he told her grimly, pulling up his zip. 'I don't ever intend putting myself back into the hell-hole of another.'

His voice was so hard-edged she could feel the bitterness emanating from him. 'What do you mean?' she queried, frowning. How could any relationship he might choose to form with a woman possibly compare with the family life that he had had?

'I've no intention of becoming a stepfather to another man's child,' he shocked her by saying. 'Even if that child *is* my niece.'

Because he didn't care about his niece's mother enough. That was what he was saying, surely?

'I don't expect you to understand. Just trust me. It would be much too complicated.'

How? she almost asked, but managed to stop herself in time. Because that would be like openly admitting that she *did* love him and *was* looking for more permanence when she wasn't, wouldn't it? she reasoned hectically. But she couldn't just leave it like that.

'Even if I was saying I wanted something more—which I'm not—but some other woman might,' she felt she ought to tag on, 'how could Daisy—or any other woman's child—complicate things?' she pressed, unable to comprehend exactly what he was saying.

He thought of his loneliness, of his mother's fear of showing any affection towards him, of the rows and the jealousies and the divided loyalties that had eventually ripped them apart.

'I mean that eventually I might want children of my own. And closer blood ties are bound to create favouritism—jealousies. How could I be sure someone else's child wouldn't take second place to my own? Or I might try too hard not to let that happen and wind up being unfair to my own offspring. I'll marry eventually, but I'll never risk becoming the kind of father my stepfather was to me.'

You aren't that kind of person, she wanted to say, but he'd think she was only hankering after marriage if she did. Instead, wanting genuinely to know, she asked tentatively, 'Are you perhaps worrying that you might follow him in other ways? That because of your upbringing you might wind up...' she was having difficulty saying it but she pressed on anyway '…wind up treating your wife and children in the same way he treated you and your mother?'

'By being physically brutal?' he supplied, looking appalled, not seeming to notice the way she winced as he said it. 'No. I abhor violence,' he appended, and from the way his firm mouth contorted she could tell he meant it—with a vengeance. 'I don't think there's a situation on earth that can't be resolved with diplomacy and communication. But a child needs its own father, and if it hasn't got that then nothing in the world is worth supplying what could only be a poor substitute.'

He meant that too, she realised, only fully understanding now, from the intensity with which he spoke, just how deeply his childhood had scarred him. But a poor substitute for what? she wondered bitterly. For a man who shrieked at his child until she screamed from the terror of it? For a man who flew into rages until she was afraid to take her baby home?

'Not that it affects me in any way,' she murmured, her throat raw from the anguish of remembering, 'but from a man of your obvious intelligence isn't that a rather short-sighted view? Do you imagine that every stepfamily in the land is suffering agonies of torment just because yours did? That every child who loses a parent—for whatever reason—shouldn't have the right to expect a loving surrogate father or mother in their place?'

'No,' he said, breathing out heavily through his nostrils. 'What I'm saying is that it wouldn't work for *me*. And if you think that's a rather short-sighted view—well, I'm afraid it's the only one I've got.'

Which was just unfortunate for her, Sienna thought, if she had been pinning her hopes on a wedding ring. Nevertheless she was hurting—but for him too, because he sounded so bitter, his voice harsh from the unforgettable misery of his childhood.

'Supposing one day you meet someone you really fall in love with and she has a child—or children?'

'It won't happen.' His tone was inexorable.

'How can you be so sure?'

'Because I'd be careful not to get involved with her in the first place.'

'What about me?' she ventured, trying to sound casual in spite of everything. 'Weren't you just a little bit worried that you might find yourself getting involved with me?'

'Not in that way,' he stated, and every syllable he uttered seemed to lacerate her heart.

'And what way is that?' she quizzed, swallowing emotion, unable to help the feeling that she was bleeding inside. For her being *involved* with someone could only mean being in love.

'I mean not with wedding bells and confetti and happy ever afters, Sienna. And if you've been imagining that that's where we were headed, then I'm truly sorry if I misled you.'

'No, you didn't,' she replied, chiding herself for caring so much when he had done nothing to indicate that she was any more than just another pleasurable diversion in his life—the kind he no doubt indulged in all the time with the opposite sex. Except, unlike the more sophisticated, far more sensible women who would normally share his bed, she'd been stupid enough to fall in love with him. 'Anyway, I wasn't thinking of myself in all this,' she put in, pulling her thoughts up quickly. Even if she was the worst possible kind of romantic fool for getting herself into this situation, there was no way Conan was ever going to know about it. 'I was thinking of you.'

'Me?' A self-mocking note of laughter escaped him. 'Lose no sleep over that, my dear deluded innocent. I can assure you I'm perfectly happy.'

'No, you're not. OK, maybe you are—but with

such a closed attitude to life you're going to miss out on a lot.'

'I already did,' he reminded her tersely. 'And it isn't an experience I intend repeating with any other child. If my view doesn't particularly correlate with yours, all I can say is that—like you—I'm not merely thinking of myself in all this. I'm thinking of the wider picture and the family I ultimately make myself responsible for. Daisy's my niece,' he continued pragmatically. 'Nothing will ever change that. And as my niece I'll encourage and support her and see that she never wants for anything—if you'll allow me to do that—but I won't take on the role of a father in her eyes, and I sincerely hope that you haven't given her any reason to suspect I would.'

Hurting, angry, Sienna shot back in protest. 'I've done no such thing! I told you—I've got no intention of settling down with anyone!'

'Good. Then let's keep it that way. I won't ever try to step into Niall's shoes, or presume to imagine that I could give Daisy—or any other man's child for that matter—the understanding and emotional stability that only her own father could have given her.'

Which was a joke in itself, Sienna thought bitterly, resisting the urge to tell him just how 'emotionally stable' his younger brother had been.

'And if you're still harbouring any ideas about pitying me, then you can dispense with them now. If you'd lived through the undesirable set-up I lived through, you'd realise that I'm being totally practical.'

'That's not being practical, Conan,' she advised, realising how strongly he believed it. 'That's being afraid.'

'Call it what you like. The subject isn't open for any more discussion,' he stated harshly, and his coldness and then the slamming of the bathroom door hurt her almost as much as the first time Niall had hit her.

CHAPTER TEN

CONAN came out of the villa carrying Sienna's and Daisy's cases. The morning was still and warm, with a mist lying over the distant mountains, but the sun shining on the water beyond the terraced gardens was making it appear piercingly blue.

The boot of the Mercedes was open, where his chauffeur had been loading his own luggage earlier, but at the moment he could only see Sienna tossing her jacket onto the rear seat of the car.

He knew he had hurt her by making his intentions clear, even if she had seemed quite adamant about not making a commitment herself. Whether she was simply bluffing or whether she meant it, he still wasn't sure. He just hadn't wanted her thinking that he was intending to settle down and play happy families when he clearly wasn't. However, that still didn't stop him feeling like a first-rate heel. A feeling only made worse as he remembered how she had refused to take any of the money he had promised her for coming here when he had offered it to her recently, and how she had firmly re-buffed any suggestion of his buying her a new car.

Daisy was still inside, saying her last goodbyes to Claudette and the staff, and so, grabbing this precious last chance to be alone with Sienna for heaven knew how long, Conan quickened his stride past the marble columns above the steps.

She was leaning with her bent arms resting on the roof of his car. The short yellow dress she was wearing with simple black pumps—which was no doubt from a high street store—did as much, if not more for her in its chic simplicity, he decided, than any of the expensive designs she had obvi-ously worn to please his brother.

She hadn't heard him approaching, giving him time to enjoy the quiet pleasure of admiring her.

With silent masculine appreciation he took in the swanlike elegance of her neck beneath the shin-ing dark cap of her hair, the way the flattering cut of the dress left one arm and shoulder completely bare, that delicate butterfly design on her silken skin.

He'd always disliked tattoos, and yet this one somehow seemed to underline the intrinsic gentle-ness in her character—as though its subject had actually chosen to settle there and was feeling too safe to fly away.

Impatient with himself for indulging in such sentimental codswallop, he gave himself a mental shake, and from just a few yards away said coolly, without any preamble, 'You've been avoiding me.' And wound up berating himself for catching her off-guard when she swung round, startled, because that was what he had been intending.

'No, I haven't,' she responded cagily, looking up at him with one slender hand shielding her eyes.

But she had been, he assured himself. She had made sure of involving herself with whatever it was Daisy and Avril had been doing all the previous afternoon and evening, before she'd taken herself off to bed early under the pretext, he was sure, of having a headache. And he was certain that she'd only been pretending to be asleep when he'd looked into her room after knocking quietly on her door.

'I'm sorry if what we were discussing yesterday upset you.' He felt uncomfortable bringing it up. But why on earth should he? he wondered, lifting each heavy individual suitcase with remarkable ease into the boot.

Was he sorry? Sienna viewed him guardedly. Sporting that dark executive image—he'd said he had a business meeting to attend as soon as they touched down in London—and with the sunlight striking brilliance from the glittering gold of his eyes, he looked anything but penitent.

'It didn't.' Her smile was forced. How could he still take her breath away when she now knew what he had been open enough to warn her of in his bedroom yesterday? There was absolutely no future for them. Not that she had been expecting that there would be, but it still hadn't stopped it hurting to have him spell it out. 'I'm made of sterner stuff than to fall apart merely by being told the truth,' she told him, brazening it out. Taking a deep breath, she asked far more lightly than she was feeling, 'So what happens now?'

'You tell me. If you wish it, there's no reason why we shouldn't carry on as we are.'

So he'd really meant that yesterday, about not ending what they had. They could still carry on having great sex just so long as she realised that for him it didn't mean anything other than that.

With her heart giving an almost painful lurch, she echoed breathlessly, 'Carry on…?'

'I don't see why not. But it has to be your decision.'

Because he could just walk away from her without turning a hair, seeing her as just another satisfying interlude in his life, while she…

She would just have to grin and bear it when he *did* walk out of her life for good.

Except that it never would be for good, would it? she realised hopelessly. Because there was Daisy. Daisy who bound them both together and with whom he would naturally want to keep in touch, like the father he was determined never to be.

Turning her gaze away from him, to hide all that she was feeling, she uttered, 'And if I decide against it?'

'It would be a pity,' he exhaled, his chest lifting beneath that immaculate white shirt, 'when we seem to gel so well.'

'In bed, you mean.' He didn't answer. How could he? she thought, when in doing so he'd be admitting to reducing what there was between them to little more than an animal coupling?

'As I said, it has to be your decision. But I don't think you're ready to let go, Sienna, any more than I'm prepared to let you. You know I can't get enough of you, and you don't have to say a word for me to know that it's entirely mutual.'

'I might be weak,' she murmured, 'but I'm not a total fool.'

Like hell she wasn't! she thought, despairing of herself. If she'd listened to her head instead of her heart at the beginning she wouldn't be in the mess she was in now.

'Don't think about breaking things off between us, Sienna. Right now I need you in my life like I've never needed anyone.' Where had *that* come from? he asked himself, wondering how he could possibly have allowed any woman to impel him to admit a thing like that—let alone the woman against whom he had harboured a three year long grievance, and a desire to teach her a lesson without any regard for what the cost might be. 'Right now you're good for me—we're good for each other,' he appended, thinking how selfish he was in danger of sounding. But there wasn't a woman anywhere he felt so desperate to keep in his bed. 'Of course if you're asking me to prove it to you…'

'No!' Her hands came up to protect herself from his particular brand of persuasion as his sudden nearness and that roughness in his voice—which could only be inspired by his desire for her—called to an answering need deep down inside. All right, he had been hurt, she thought. And badly. But then so had she. And she didn't intend letting a man use her or hurt her—either physically or emotionally—ever again. Apart from which, she had Daisy to consider now. 'This isn't a very good idea,' she told him tremulously, finding it took every ounce of emotional strength she had to be able to say it. 'We had a fling. We had a good time. Let's leave it like that.' She was amazed at how nonchalant she managed to sound.

'A *fling?*' His face creased up as though he couldn't fully comprehend what she was saying. 'Is that what you want to call it?'

'Wasn't it?' she murmured, the lightness of her tone hiding the real anguish behind her words.

Something hardened his jaw and he started to say something, but was stalled by the sound of childish chatter.

They both looked up as the little girl came skipping out of the house ahead of her grandmother. Carefully negotiating the steps, she ran straight up to Conan and held up her hippo.

'I told him we were going home, but he says he wants to stay with you,' she told him breathlessly, the innocent little gesture striking at Sienna's heart.

'No, Daisy,' she advised firmly, guessing just what Conan would think of that. 'Uncle Conan's coming back to England anyway, so Hippo's only going to be lonely.'

'No, he won't!' Daisy remonstrated, sticking out her bottom lip. 'He says he wants to stay until he comes back.'

'I said no, Daisy…'

The little girl squealed in protest, shrugging off Sienna's hand.

'Let her leave it if she wants to.'

Conan's voice cut impatiently across the altercation between mother and daughter, leaving Sienna wondering, after they had said their goodbyes to Avril and were on the open road, whether his off-handedness sprang from his niece's innocent attempts to squeeze her way into his affections, or from her own refusal to continue an affair that was going nowhere.

She had been back at the gym for a couple of weeks, juggling her courses with Daisy's new schooling schedule and trying to keep her mind off Conan by plunging herself into the daily reward of helping others—particularly her older class members—to reach healthier levels of fitness, when he suddenly turned up out of the blue.

It was a Thursday, which she remembered telling him once was usually her morning off. What she hadn't reckoned on was that he would remember that.

It was with a surprised leap of her heart therefore, after coming back from dropping Daisy off and taking a shower, that she padded to the front door in her short cotton robe to find him standing there on the step.

'Conan!'

Impeccably groomed as always, power-dressed in his dark executive suit, he made her feel at an immediate disadvantage, with her hair still damp and dishevelled, and far too conscious of being totally naked under her robe.

'Hello, Sienna,' he said, against a backing of excited barks. 'May I come in?'

She pressed herself back against the door, and as he stepped in was reminded of the first time he had come here. Except now he stooped to pet Shadow, who had rushed in from the garden at the first peal of the doorbell, no longer viewing the dog as a cold reminder of that dreadful attack he had suffered in the past. But as he moved past her, with that evocative scent of cologne almost spelling his signature, she was far too aware that—unlike that first time he had come here—he now knew every secret pathway of her body; knew just what to do to make it respond with shameless abandon to his irresistible masculinity. Just as it was doing now—and without any help from him!

'How's Daisy?' he asked, before she had gathered herself enough to say anything.

'She's fine.' Searching for words, so that he

wouldn't guess how his dark allure was making her breasts ache and making that familiar heat at the heart of her pool into honeyed moistness in unwitting preparation for his hard invasion, she added croakily, 'So, to what do I owe this unexpected visit?'

An elevated eyebrow acknowledged the tremor that destabilised her voice as he held back for her to precede him into the living room, his manners impeccable as always.

'I wanted to let you know that Avril's well enough to return to London and will be moving into her new apartment within the next couple of weeks,' he informed her smoothly, with no sign apparent of the kind of upheaval going on inside Sienna. It was an apartment that Conan was buying his mother especially to make it easier for her to see Daisy, she remembered Avril telling her before they had left France.

'You could have phoned.' She said it too curtly, and wondered if he could sense the panic that was rising in her.

'I could have.' His eyes were resting on hers— probing, too discerning—before they slid to the betraying movement of her rapidly rising breasts. 'I've missed you, Sienna.'

Through an escalating tension she was aware of Shadow padding back out to the garden.

And I haven't missed you?

With her body turning weak from the velvety caress of his voice, she couldn't tell him how she couldn't keep her mind on anything. That all she could see was his face swimming in front of her eyes every minute of every day. And that she woke up in the night aching for his loving and had to get up and walk about, make herself tea she didn't want to stop herself succumbing to humiliating and unfulfilling self-release.

'Don't!' She made to sweep away from him, put some distance between them, but strong fingers were suddenly clamping around her wrist.

'Sienna…'

'It's over,' she breathed, panic showing in her eyes as electricity crackled through her from the sensuous agony of his touch.

'No, it isn't.'

His determination outstripped any protest she might have made as his other hand reached up and tugged gently on the belt of her robe.

The garment fell open, leaving her exposed and vulnerable.

A tense heat radiated through her and she pressed her eyes tightly closed, feeling his gaze like a hot brand as he groaned in satisfied acknowledgment of her body's shameless betrayal. 'You still want me, Sienna,' he said deeply. 'Every bit as much as I want you.'

Even now, as his hand slid up around one burgeoning breast and her body arched involuntarily towards him, she wanted to deny it. But it was only her head she was trying to fool, because as his mouth came down over hers her physical responses were telling her something else entirely.

Dear heaven! How long had it been?

Her arms went joyously around him, her body glorying in its triumph over her brain, her pulsing flesh exulting in the recognition of its master, its dark, exciting Svengali, whose command it craved to obey.

'You can't give this up any more than I can, can you?' He broke their kiss to speak breathlessly, not needing to hear her answer because her instinctive responses said it all. 'So why did you think you could?'

His voice was rough and ragged, his mouth and hands moving urgently over her body as though not knowing which part of her to savour first. But her need for him was just as desperate, her laboured breathing coming just as rapidly as his, her hungry fingers tugging at his shirt, pulling it out of his waistband so that she could slip her hands beneath it and feel the throbbing heat of his sinewy body before he lifted her up, with her legs entwined around him, and carried her in a few purposeful strides across the room.

They made love on her old wooden table, amongst the debris of unironed washing, pending bills and a box bursting with Daisy's toys. It was a quick, hot, urgent coming together, but neither of them wanted anything else, both driven by the only thing that mattered right then, which was the swift, hard locking of bodies in an immediate climax so intense that Sienna cried out from the blistering pleasure of it, feeling the tremors that ran through Conan from the hard propulsion of his body until he gave a shuddering groan as he found his own release and collapsed heavily down on top of her.

A little later, as their breathing returned to normal, she said—surprisingly shyly in the circumstances, 'You came prepared.' Because even in their uncontrollable need for each other he had taken effortless time to protect her.

'Around you I can't afford to do anything else,' he responded with a wry grimace as he brought himself up on his elbows, then carefully withdrew from her.

Of course he wouldn't want to make her pregnant and risk finding himself in the sort of family situation he despised. Which was slap-bang in the midst of another stepfamily, she realised, if he did what he would probably consider to be his duty and married her. Which she wouldn't agree to anyway, she thought wretchedly—even if she hadn't had that bad experience with Niall—because there was no way that she'd be prepared to marry a man who resented having to take on Daisy, however strong his reasons were for not doing so, any more than she'd be prepared to marry a man whose only reason for marrying her was because she was having his child.

'Conan…' With her forehead creasing from the effort, she tried to tell him that this was all a mistake. That she hadn't intended to make love with him and that the decision she'd made in France had been the right one. But the unintentional brush of his fingers against her inner thigh as he inspected the condom caused her breath to catch—which he capitalised on by turning the back of his hand against the still swollen bud of her femininity until she started to writhe against him, effectively silenced as his long skilled fingers did his bidding and tipped her over the brink for a second time, because he had known instinctively what she had been going to say.

'Better get dressed,' he whispered when it was over, pressing a feather-light kiss on her nose, drawing her attention to the fact that she was as good as naked while he had done very little more than unzip his trousers and loosen his tie. 'You're far too much of a temptation looking like this.'

A temptation to do what? See how many more times he could get her to capitulate? she demanded of herself, noting that dark satisfaction in his voice. To have her bucking at his command, knowing that having sex with him was going against everything she'd made up her mind not to do? Because that was all it was to him, she thought fervently, scrambling up off the table and fastening her robe around her. Just sex.

Hurting and ashamed, berating herself for being too weak to resist him, and annoyed with him for reducing her to such a quivering mass of need, before she knew it she was flinging at him, 'And you're far too much of an arrogant swine to take no for an answer!'

Anger leaped like green fire in his eyes, but was quickly brought under control by his daunting self-command.

'I wasn't aware that what has happened between us here was anything but mutual,' he rasped in a dangerously soft voice, and she could tell that he was only just managing to hold his anger in check. 'You're as hooked as I am, Sienna, so don't blame me if that doesn't tie in with your misplaced delusions of innocence in all this. You made love with me because you wanted to. Because where you and I are concerned you can't help yourself any more than I can! And if you think I'm proud of myself for getting us both into this situation, then I can assure you categorically, darling, I'm *not!*'

Smarting from his words, shamed by her statement which had provoked them, she stood tensely, wishing she could retract it as he brushed past her and moved out to the minute little room off the kitchen that housed her small downstairs bathroom, telling herself that he had every right to be angry.

Because of course what she had been accusing him of was his failure to respect the decision she had made in France about not continuing an affair with him. But because of her frustration with herself for falling into his arms the minute he arrived, it had come out sounding like something far, far worse. With just that one remark she had relegated him to the worst kind of man imaginable. The type who bullied and bulldozed his way into a woman's bed. Like his stepfather had with his mother. Like Niall.

She shivered as the memory of her marriage came back with shuddering force. She'd thought the past was over—done with. And it was, she assured herself rationally. It was just that sometimes things happened to bring it all back…

A familiar clunk from beyond the kitchen had her darting through to investigate.

Conan had just emerged from the bathroom, pulling the door closed behind him. As she'd expected, the loose handle, with its spindle still attached, had come clean off in his hand.

'The one on the bathroom side keeps dropping off,' she uttered by way of apology for her shabby little home, thinking how devastatingly sophisticated he appeared in her modest little kitchen—which certainly wasn't the place for an enterprising self-made billionaire. 'I bought some screws on the way home this morning. I was going to try and fix it when I had a minute.'

'Then give them to me.'

She wanted to tell him that it was all right—that she didn't need anyone to help her. But he was already taking off his jacket, so she went and fetched the packet of screws that was still in her handbag in the living room. When she came back he was repositioning the handle on the bathroom side, and she tried not to notice how his skin showed bronze through the fine white shirt as she handed him the screwdriver from the kitchen drawer.

As he worked he didn't seem to care that he was kneeling in his best designer trousers, or that he was in danger of scuffing his expensive hand-made shoes on her rather worn quarry-tiled floor.

Perhaps he wasn't too sophisticated to be able to fit in anywhere, she decided, admiring him, her heart swelling involuntarily, noticing how the morning sun shining through the kitchen window seemed to strike fire from his gleaming hair. She restrained the strongest urge to run her fingers through it, deciding that that would betray far too much of what she was feeling and might make him think she was getting serious about him. Which was crazy, she thought, after all the intimacies they had shared.

'There.' He was trying the door handle he had just fixed, making sure it was working properly. 'That should do the trick.' His personal masculine scent impinged on her senses as he got to his feet.

'Thanks.' She watched him secure the packet of remaining screws before putting them with the screwdriver back into the drawer. A neat and tidy workman, just like her father, she decided. And, just like her father, a man who would never hurt her. Not physically anyway. Only emotionally, she thought. And only then if she allowed him to. But she wasn't going to, was she? she tried convincing herself. Even so, her throat felt raw with emotion as she uttered tentatively, 'What I said earlier...' He was shrugging back into his jacket, his eyes dark and inscrutable, and she knew that deep down he was still angry with her for saying what she had. 'I didn't mean it like it sounded. I only meant—'

A broad thumb against her lips cut short what she had been trying to tell him. 'I think we've both said enough for one day.'

The next second she was in his arms, with her cheek pressed against his jacket, her hand moving in an involuntary caress over the soft fabric of his sleeve. One steely arm was tightening with torturous possession around her middle, the other a clamping bar that lay diagonally across her back.

They were as one, she thought, enlivened by the power and the strength and the warmth of him. Joined at the chest and the hip and the thigh, her pelvis pressing with equal possession against his, drawn like a magnet to his hard masculinity, while her head swam with his scent and her heart beat out a message that she feared he wouldn't fail to hear.

I love you!

She bit back the phrase that sprang too easily to

her lips, knowing the words would be anathema to him after what he had told her that day at the villa. He was quite prepared for them to carry on as lovers, but that there could never be any future for them. He'd never be a stepfather to Daisy, or any other man's child for that matter, because of the violence he'd witnessed by his stepfather towards his mother, and because of the ridicule and brutality directed at him by the man who had shaped his early life.

Aching for him almost as much as she was aching for herself, she wanted to blurt out that she understood all the fear and misery that he must have gone through. That she had experienced the same sort of fear and misery herself. But what good would it do? she thought. The past was gone—as she had reminded herself earlier. So what benefit would it be to Conan to drag it all up? He knew that his mother was weak and his stepfather had been brutal. How could she destroy Niall's image so completely in his eyes by telling him that the brother he'd loved had not only been weak—which he already knew—but that he had been afflicted with the same brutal streak? She couldn't. Any more than he could forget the past and even think about building a happy, normal relationship with someone like her and Daisy.

All she could do, she decided, trying to drum up the strength, was tell him that she was sticking to the decision she had made in France—which was that she had no intention of sleeping with him again.

And she would have done it, too, she assured herself, if his pager hadn't bleeped at the exact moment she decided to.

'I'm sorry about this.' He grimaced, releasing her so that he could take the call.

Which was curt, brief and to the point. He was needed and he had to go.

'I'll be in touch,' he promised, touching her mouth fleetingly with his.

A few moments later she heard the powerful car growling away, leaving her frustrated and despairing with herself for not telling him when she had had the chance.

CHAPTER ELEVEN

SIENNA had been determined to finish with Conan after that last time he had called, when they had wound up making love on her sitting room table. But that was easier said than done, she'd soon discovered, when she was drawn to him physically in a way that defied all rational argument, and when emotionally she was head over heels in love with him, even while her head kept warning her of the hopelessness of the situation.

Because when he'd called the next time—aware that his niece was off on a school trip—and taken her out for a lunch she had been too weak to refuse, and then the time after that, when he'd dropped Daisy off at her grandmother's and whisked Sienna to an exhibition by her favourite artist that she had been longing to attend, on both occasions he'd brought her back to the house and they had inevitably wound up making love.

Now, hearing his car purring away after another abandoned hour of paradise with him on her little single bed, Sienna tugged her duvet straight with intensifying annoyance at herself as common sense reminded her that if she was stupid enough to imagine that he might suddenly have a change of mind-set and want a long-term relationship with her—and consequently Daisy—then she was just living in cloud-cuckoo-land. Apart from which, she reminded herself with increasing self-recrimination, she didn't just have her own feelings to consider, but Daisy's.

The little girl had become extremely attached to him, and was continually asking Sienna when he was coming round. But she knew for a fact that when he did pick Daisy up to take her to see Avril he was merely acting as a go-between for his mother and his little niece. He seldom stayed to spend that much time with Daisy. And when he did eventually bring her home, having bought her ice cream, a book of animal stories or various other treats he obviously thought a caring uncle should provide, Daisy never wanted to see him leave— something that had started to spark off tantrums the minute he did.

Sienna was glad, therefore, when towards the end of September he went away for three weeks, tied up with the potential take-over of a floundering communications network in Europe. It gave her some space to think, although it wasn't easy being left to question the inadvisability of what she was doing—for her own sake as well as Daisy's—when another part of her—the part that wouldn't listen to reason—was aching for him with a need that was almost unbearable.

Her mother rang a couple of times while he was away, fishing for any whiff of intimacy between Conan Ryder and her daughter. Sienna knew her mother would have loved to be able to tell her friends that her daughter was romantically in-volved with the illustrious billionaire, but managed to stay firmly non-committal. Jodie's questions, however, weren't so easy to evade when she came round to show off her new baby boy.

'He comes to see Daisy,' Sienna dissembled, when her friend teasingly remarked upon the num-ber of times she had seen the BMW parked out-side the house.

'Even when she isn't here?' Jodie responded knowingly.

Which just went to show how dishonestly her relationship with Conan was making her behave, Sienna realised, rebuking herself. Not only with her friend, but with her own daughter! Because she had made sure from the outset that Daisy didn't get to know that she was sleeping with Conan—

something that Conan himself had had no problem going along with. After all, he had exercised the same discretion in France, she remembered, although it wasn't until after he had warned her not to fall in love with him that day at the villa that she had realised why. He didn't want his niece seeing him as anything more than the dutiful uncle he was—least of all as a potential father!

Well, that's all right by me! Sienna thought grittily, forcing herself to see what a complete idiot she was being in allowing him to use her in the way he was—although that didn't stop her impulses going into immediate overdrive the following day when he telephoned to let her know he was back.

She was expecting to see him on her own when he came round that Thursday morning, but an unexpected school closure for some emergency repairs had found her having to delegate her afternoon's training sessions at the gym. It also meant that Daisy was there when he called.

'Let me take you both out,' he suggested generously, spectacularly clad in dark jeans and a black leather jacket, and concealing any disappointment he might have felt—if he was harbouring any.

Reluctantly Sienna agreed, and wasn't sure afterwards whether he'd really enjoyed being in the pet and aquatic centre that he took them to, or whether he had just been making the best of it, when what he had really intended that morning was to have her alone, naked and in bed. Something his eyes told her he still wanted every time they met hers over Daisy's oblivious little head, and which produced a throbbing response in Sienna even while she nursed a sort of torturous satisfaction from knowing he'd been denied having his own way.

It was late in the afternoon when Conan drove them back to her place. Daisy had slept most of the way home, but was her usual energetic self by the time Sienna let them all into the house, and immediately flew out into the garden after Shadow.

Shortly afterwards, having finished the coffee that Sienna had made for them both, Conan set his mug down on the draining board and moved back to her where she was standing at the kitchen counter.

Her breath seemed to lodge in her lungs as his arm snaked around her.

'I'm going to have to go,' he whispered from behind, causing her blood to race as his hand slid upwards to cup one soft responsive breast which yielded too eagerly beneath her bra and the smooth fabric of her sweatshirt. His lips inside the wide neckline sent hot and tingling sensations along her spine.

'I don't want you to go!' Daisy's torn little appeal had Sienna pivoting away from him. Too late, she realised, because her daughter had already seen everything. 'I don't want you to go!' the little girl reiterated passionately, already starting to cry, and Sienna could feel another tantrum coming on. 'Why can't you stay with us? *Why* can't you?' Daisy was sobbing bitterly as she clung to one jean-clad leg, looking up with tears streaming down her face at the man she had clearly grown to adore.

'Because I have to be somewhere else, Daisy.' Conan dropped to his haunches to talk to her.

Immediately sturdy little arms went around his neck. 'No, you don't,' her muffled little voice sobbed above the creak of his straining leather.

'Yes, I do, Daisy.' There was an odd inflexion in his voice, Sienna noted, as his arms moved tentatively around the little girl, the sight so painfully heart-wrenching that she had to turn away and busy herself with the tin of dog food she had just opened.

'Then why can't we come and live with you?'

When she turned around there was such an intensity of emotion in the eyes that lifted to hers that she felt it as tangibly as her own. What was it? she wondered achingly. Hopelessness? Desperation?

An appeal to her to get him out of this situation he had unintentionally created?

'Go and take this out to Shadow, Daisy,' she advised tremulously, holding out the dog's bowl and looking helplessly at Conan when the little girl didn't even turn around.

'Go and do as your mother wishes and then we'll talk about it, Daisy.' He spoke softly—deeply—with just enough promise in his voice to get her to comply, which after a few moments' hesitation she did.

'What the hell are you trying to do?' Sienna threw at him angrily as soon as Daisy was out of earshot.

'What do you mean, what am I trying to do?' He was upright, dominating her tiny living space again.

'Giving her reason to hope like that! She might only be four years old but she isn't an idiot! She saw us, Conan. And now she thinks we're all going to be one hunky-dory little family!'

'Then you're going to have to somehow explain to her that we're not.'

'*I'm* going to have to explain? And what am I supposed to say to her, exactly?' she demanded, refusing to acknowledge how much his last insensitive statement was affecting her. 'She's had one man in her life snatched away from her. How am I going to tell her not to get to attached to another who's likely to be disappearing at any minute?'

'What's that supposed to mean?' he challenged impatiently.

'It means,' she informed him, punching the swing bin open with unnecessary force and dropping the dog food tin inside, 'I don't want her thinking you're for real!'

'Well, of *course* I'm for real.' His eyes were incredulous as they followed her movements around the limited space. 'I'm her uncle, for goodness' sake!'

'Unfortunately she isn't old enough to compartmentalise!' The spoon she'd been using clanged noisily as she tossed it down on the stainless-steel drainer. Behind her she caught Conan's heavily released breath.

'I've told you. I can't be a father to her, Sienna— or make a lifelong commitment to you, if that's what you're intimating.'

'It isn't!' Heaven keep him from guessing that she might have ever dared to imagine that. That she had had enough of this pretence and waiting around for precious phone calls from him. Had enough of aching for him night after night. Loving him while knowing that because of his past and all the brutality he had suffered he would never, ever allow himself to love her back.

'I can't give her what my brother would have given her,' he went on, as though he hadn't heard her, 'and I won't even begin to try. You think I'm guilty of a closed mind? Well, just consider the hypothetical situation of us marrying. Daisy's *your* daughter. Yours and Niall's. You must have had plans for the way you were going to bring her up— still have those plans to teach her what's right from wrong, prepare her for adult life. Supposing I had conflicting views and we disagreed over her upbringing, or anything else she did or might want to do? Then we'd find ourselves in the unenviable situation of taking sides, and that would only lead to jealousy and animosity—or worse,' he expressed, grim-mouthed. 'And that sort of hypothetically perfect family I can do without!'

'Like yours, you mean?' Her tortured little reminder hung like a pollutant on the air between them.

'Yes, if you're so determined to press home the point,' he rasped, his nostrils flaring. 'Exactly like mine!'

'And I've told you before…every stepfamily on the planet isn't exactly like yours. Not that it affects *me* one iota…' She had to keep him believing that, and to emphasise that point she added, 'I don't want to be tied down any more than you do…but you're too ready to generalise. Every one of those families isn't always at each other's throats or…' She hesitated, still less than comfortable with describing the cruelty that had not only dogged his childhood but had tainted her short marriage. 'Or turning violent,' she got out at last.

From the way his face hardened she knew she had touched a raw nerve. 'Tell that to someone who's prepared to share your rose-tinted opinion,' he said coldly. 'And if you'll pardon me for saying so, Sienna, you're hardly in any position to judge.'

Oh, aren't I? her heart screamed bitterly, almost driven to reveal exactly what she had had to endure in being married to his brother. But it would have been a useless exercise in retaliation, she realised, which would serve no purpose but to hurt him. And only because she had been careless enough to fall in love with him, she thought miserably. But that was her problem, not his.

His problem was that he'd been shaped by the destructive jealousy and aggression that had sculpted his early life, and there was nothing she could do or say that could chisel away at those prejudices of his—because they were set in stone.

'Perhaps I just happen to have more faith in

human relationships than you do, Conan?' she told him painfully. And with all the courage she could muster pressing like a lead weight against her chest, she said, 'I don't think we should see each other like this any more.'

She almost felt the tension that ripped through his body. 'You don't mean that?' he whispered, taken aback.

No, she didn't, she agonised, clamming up, because how could she bring herself to say anything that would end this love affair with him for good?

As he moved towards her, though, her hands shot up to stave off any intention he might have of trying to change her mind. If he touched her, she wouldn't have a chance, she thought, panicking, and he knew it. 'I'm serious, Conan,' she croaked.

He drew up sharply, his mouth moving in a parody of a smile. 'You're tired. We both are,' he remarked, as though that was the answer to all their problems. 'We'll talk about this some other time.'

With his lips lightly brushing her forehead, he was gone before she could utter another word.

When he telephoned the next day she refused to see him, and when he rang again each day for the rest of that week her answer was the same. When she didn't hear from him the following week, she remembered he was away on a business trip. Then, during that week, with the half-term holiday coming up, she received a call from her parents, inviting her to Spain. With time off from the gym for Daisy's school holiday, Sienna was more than happy to accept.

At least she wouldn't be tempted to go back on her word about making a clean break with Conan—which she knew she had to do for Daisy's sake, if not her own. She knew that if it hadn't been for Daisy she wouldn't have been strong enough to do it. And she'd had to. She had to remain strong for the sake of her sanity and her self-respect. She owed herself that much at least.

But all the pep-talks in the world, which she was constantly having with herself, didn't help to lessen the pain she was suffering being without him. As it had stood she had started to despise herself for being his ready mistress whenever he took it upon himself to call her. But even that less than happy state of affairs had been preferable to this empty longing, this burning need for him that kept her awake each night and left her chastising herself as, like an automaton, appearing normal on the outside, she somehow managed to get through each day.

There was also something else worrying her, that she couldn't even bring herself to dwell on while she was in the state she was in. She was glad, therefore, when Saturday came and she could pack Daisy and Shadow into the car.

Her cell phone rang just as they were leaving for the airport. Fortunately she was just passing a retail park, and pulled off the main highway to answer it.

'Sienna?' Conan's voice at the end of the line sent her mind into chaos. 'Sienna, don't hang up on me. I want to see you. We need to talk.'

'There isn't anything to talk about,' she protested, wishing he would leave her to recover from the pain of loving him, even while her body was turning traitor on her, forcing her to remember the insurmountable pleasure of being his. 'I can't talk right now anyway. I'm going away. I need some space.'

'I know what you need—what we both need,' he stated firmly. 'And it isn't space.'

Sienna sucked in her breath as every erogenous cell in her body reacted to the stimulus of his words just at his incredible voice. 'I've got to get going.' Her own voice cracked under the weight of her hopeless feelings for him. 'We're going to be late.'

'Where are you going anyway?' he demanded, controlled and authoritative in comparison.

'If you must know we're going to Spain!'

Behind her an excited Daisy was kicking her legs against her car seat, asking to speak to her uncle. It didn't help either that Shadow, catching the familiar tones of the disembodied voice, was leaning through the gap in the seat and panting into her left ear.

'No, Daisy. Not now!' Regretting her impulse to snap at the little girl, Sienna had to bite her tongue to stop herself telling Conan to leave her alone—to leave them all alone. He had ties with Daisy and always would have, she reminded herself ruefully, knowing she should have given far more thought to this situation before she had gone so eagerly into his bed.

'It sounds like you've got your hands full. Why don't I come and meet you at the airport?'

'For what reason, Conan?'

From the deep breath she heard him draw he was clearly becoming impatient. 'For the simple reason that I'd like to see my niece.'

Of course. What was she expecting him to say? That he loved her? That the past couple of weeks had been torture and that he couldn't live without her? There was a painful little twist to her mouth as she told him, 'Then you'll just have to wait until she gets back. Now, if you don't mind, I've got a plane to catch so I can start to get on with my life!'

'And that's really how you feel?'

No, I want you, and I can never have you! she agonised silently. Bravely, though, with her shoulders drawn back, she murmured into the mouthpiece, 'That's how I feel.'

At the other end of the line, Conan took another deep breath and held it. She wanted to get on with her life, she'd said, and what right did he have to try and stop her? None whatsoever, his conscience told him, even if he couldn't bear the thought of her sleeping with any other man.

There was no future for them and he'd known it from the start. He just hadn't listened to the voice of reason when it had told him how awkward sleeping with his niece's mother would make things for them in the long term. He had wanted Sienna too much for that. He guessed now that he would just have to arrange for his chauffeur to pick up Daisy whenever he or her grandmother planned to see her. That wouldn't be too difficult, and at least it would mean that his and Sienna's paths wouldn't cross, which surely was the most sensible thing all round. It was time to let her go.

That decision made, it was in a tone devoid of any emotion that he breathed into the phone he was gripping with a tension that surprised him, 'Then goodbye, Sienna.' The click as he cut them off signalled the end of an era.

Sienna stared at her phone as though it was something she had never seen before, let alone just used to terminate her affair with the only man she knew now she had ever truly loved.

Harrowed and shocked, she willed him to ring back, so she could tell him that she hadn't meant it. That she didn't want to get on with a life when he wasn't in it. But the plain and simple truth was that she had to. Wasn't that why she'd allowed the argument to take the turn it had? Wasn't it better that they ended the affair now, when they could both walk away with their dignity intact, rather than at some later date when Conan, having tired of her and started seeking new pastures, walked away under his own steam, leaving her dignity in tatters?

Except that right then she didn't care about her dignity or her self-respect, because the ache that spread outwards from the region of her heart seemed to be suffocating her.

Emotion welled up in her until she could scarcely draw breath and the busy car park in front of her was nothing but a blur.

She had to breathe. Focus on that, she thought.

She was wondering how she was going to keep from breaking down in front of Daisy—until a little voice piped up from the back seat, 'Mummy, I want to go to the toilet.'

She was grateful for that mundane demand that made her focus on something else. Her responsibilities. Not this stifling and all-consuming agony that she knew would take her over if she let it.

'All right, darling.'

That duty discharged, she led Daisy back from the public conveniences and told her to stand beside her and not move while she got the orange juice that the little girl had been asking for out of the boot.

Rummaging in her bag, and then in the pocket of her casual jacket, it hit her suddenly that she had been so wound up over Conan when she had got out of the car that not only had she forgotten to lock it, she had even left her keys in the ignition!

Berating herself for her carelessness, she was only half aware of a dog barking somewhere in another vehicle as she opened her door to retrieve them. What she didn't expect was for Shadow to come leaping over her seat, nearly knocking her off-balance as he shot out of the car and went haring off across the tarmac.

The only thought in her mind to strap Daisy

safely in the car, so that she could go after the dog, Sienna spun round—to meet every mother's worst nightmare.

The little girl who had been standing beside her less than half a second ago had darted out after Shadow into the busy car park.

'Daisy!' Sienna screamed, her feet flying as she tried to reach her. But, too late, life suddenly took on the aspect of some horrifying dream.

Almost in slow motion, it seemed, she saw the wheels of the brake-screeching four-by-four skidding on the wet tarmac, and then the little figure in the red anorak and pale leggings went down before her eyes.

CHAPTER TWELVE

CONAN felt as though he had been sitting there in that hospital ward for days, when in fact it must only have been a matter of hours.

When Sienna had rung him, sounding almost hysterical, at first he hadn't been able to grasp what she was saying. When he had, a dread had taken hold of him such as he had never experienced before, immobilising him, rendering him speechless, unable to think.

He who could turn vast corporations around, who had been clear-headed enough to build a commercial empire from next to nothing, had suddenly been thrown into chaos. One minute he had been arguing with Sienna on the phone and the next she was ringing to say that Daisy had had an accident and was being rushed to the hospital. And when she'd managed to tell him what had happened he'd found himself praying as he'd never prayed in his life.

Not Daisy! he had heard himself silently begging. *Please! Not Daisy!* He'd been tortured then by all the chances he had had to show the little girl his affection and hadn't, when she had shown him so much. Like climbing on his knee when he'd reluctantly agreed to read her a story. Like leaving him her precious hippo. Like clinging to him, sobbing, that last time he had seen her because she hadn't wanted him to go. *You've taken Niall!* he'd thundered silently to anyone who might have been listening, battling with anger, guilt and a cold, overriding fear. *Isn't that enough? Or won't you be satisfied until you've taken Daisy too?*

Except that the four-by-four hadn't hit her, as they had at first feared, he reflected now with agonising relief, although no one could believe how it had managed to miss her. It had been tripping over a kerbstone and banging her head on the ground that had left her worryingly concussed. But even that frightening interlude was over now, because she had regained full consciousness not long after he'd arrived at the hospital and, with thorough tests revealing no other serious injuries, she was sleeping quite normally.

'She's going to be fine.' From the other side of the bed, Sienna almost mouthed the words across the little slumbering form, her smile tremulous, her moist eyes tired and dark, her face racked with the same pained relief that he was feeling.

He nodded, but didn't say anything, tension clamping his jaw as he turned away, battling with the welling of emotion.

He had taken off his jacket and tie earlier, and unfastened the top button of his shirt. His hair was dishevelled from where he had been raking his fingers through it, Sienna noticed. His chin was heavily shadowed with a day's growth of stubble, and his rugged features appeared so lined that he seemed to have aged five years since she had seen him last. But then he'd been worrying about Daisy, she thought. After all, she was his brother's child. And in that moment she was immensely grateful that she had never had to tell him the truth about Niall.

'The nurse I spoke to on my way in here thought she was my daughter,' he imparted in an oddly gruff voice.

Because of their shared surname, Sienna realised. It was a natural mistake to make.

Doing her best to hide the anguish of his crushing, final goodbye over the phone, before this awful thing had happened to Daisy, with an ironic little twist to her mouth, she murmured, 'I hope you put them straight.'

Again he didn't answer—but then neither did she expect him to. He was just being considerate in not telling her he had after all she had been through this evening, she thought, closing her eyes against the pain of ultimately losing him.

Sienna had telephoned her parents earlier, to tell them what had happened, and Faith Swann had been almost hysterical, insisting on flying over from Spain immediately. Conan had arranged for them to be flown over in one of his private jets, and they'd arrived in the early hours, her mother crying with relief to know that her granddaughter was going to be all right, her father fishing for his handkerchief before turning away, saying he had something in his eye.

Conan had also arranged for them to be put up in one of the best hotels near the hospital, putting a car and driver at their disposal so that they wouldn't have to worry about getting around while they were in England. Just as effortlessly, Sienna remembered, he'd arranged for someone to pick up her car from that car park, along with Shadow who, having returned, had been lying dutifully beside her when the ambulance arrived, and was now being looked after by a member of Conan's staff in the exclusive penthouse apartment he occupied when he was in town.

'Conan hasn't been able to do enough for us. And all at his own expense!' her mother crooned, enjoying dropping his name for the benefit of a nurse who had just come to check on Daisy. 'Which tells me that he's more than a little bit interested in you, Sienna.'

Sienna pretended to smile, fixing her gaze on the pink patterned curtain that hung beside Daisy's bed so that no one would see the raw emotion slashing her face.

The hospital discharged Daisy that afternoon.

Conan had left earlier, called back to his office by some business only he could sanction, and Sienna couldn't help wondering whether, now that he knew Daisy was going to be all right, he'd felt relieved to get away. After all, he wouldn't want any further complications with his niece's mother.

Faith and Barry Swann had already left the ward with their granddaughter a few minutes ago. Now, checking there was nothing of Daisy's left in the room, Sienna swung the holdall her parents had brought in with fresh clothes for them both over her shoulder and took the lift down to the ground floor, trying not to think about Conan and how empty her life was going to be without him, or even how she was going to cope, although she knew she had to. Had to hang on to that self-sufficiency she prized—especially in the light of what that shockingly revealing test she had done two days ago had confirmed.

Her parents weren't actually waiting for her in Reception, as expected, but *he* was, and Sienna's legs seemed to turn to mush as he looked up and saw her.

Tall and imposing, he had freshened up in the short time he had been gone, and his dark physical presence was utterly mind-blowing.

In black jeans and a grey, white and black multi-striped shirt, with his clean, sleek black hair just brushing his collar, he exuded a lethal blend of ruggedness and sophistication that no woman—herself included, Sienna thought hopelessly—could ever hope to resist.

'Conan!'

Her anguished sapphire gaze locked with the green-gold of his, and there was such dark emotion beneath the black fringes of his lashes that her heart seemed to stop from the intensity of it.

Nothing in his tone, however, revealed what he was thinking as he said, 'I gather the little invalid's been pronounced fit enough to leave?' When she nodded, he asked, 'What about you?'

'I'm fine,' she murmured, although having nearly

lost her precious little daughter last night she was feeling anything but. Yet he'd been there too, she remembered, sharing every minute of those worrying hours with her after Daisy had been brought in. And through the night they'd kept up an almost silent vigil beside her bed. Like parents, she thought achingly, united in their worry and their love for a child they had created—longed for— though in reality nothing could have been further from the truth.

'You don't look it,' he said.

'Neither do you.'

He had shaved since she had last seen him, though there were still dark shadows under his eyes. And although he was casually dressed, and looking coolly magnificent, she sensed an air about him that was far from relaxed—like a caged animal wanting to be free.

Which was exactly what he was, she realised, harrowed.

'I can manage,' she protested, as he relieved her of the holdall.

He merely indicated for her to precede him through the sliding doors.

Sienna didn't argue, because that cedarwood scent of him was enervating, and because when his sleeve had brushed her arm just then it had sent a flood of torturous memories coursing through her. Making love with him on his yacht, the boat a white pearl against the blue water. Being worshipped like a goddess on the table in that vast kitchen in the villa. Lying naked on his bed and provoking him with that glass of wine until his control had snapped.

Outside the day was gentle, with the mellow warmth of autumn, and a golden sun was shining through a gap between the buildings on the other side of the busy road, making even the concrete city look kind.

'Where are Mum and Dad?' she asked, looking towards the parking bays for the Mercedes and the chauffeur he had provided them with.

'They've gone ahead with Daisy. I assured them I would see you got home safely,' he said.

Which would have pleased Faith Swann immensely, Sienna decided, guessing that his popularity couldn't go up any more notches with her mother if he had tried.

'Why?' she demanded, hurting, but he didn't respond as he guided her across the tarmac to where his car was park.

The BMW shut out the world as Conan closed the passenger door and came around the bonnet, a secure and achingly familiar bubble of luxury that was exclusively his.

He didn't say anything to her as he steered the big car through the London traffic. Perhaps he knew she didn't want to converse, she considered. Or maybe he was just thinking that everything had been said.

'Where are we going?' Lost in her thoughts, she didn't notice the slip road for her suburb until they'd cruised past it.

'We have to talk,' Conan said.

She darted him a glance, her forehead puckering. 'What about?' Her stomach started churning queasily.

'We didn't part very amicably over the phone yesterday. And then what happened afterwards...' He cast his eyes across the space between them. 'I can't help feeling that I somehow managed to contribute to it in some way.'

By saying goodbye?

If he meant she'd left her keys in her car, which had set off the train of events that had led to Daisy's accident, because she hadn't had her mind on what she was doing—something she'd been rebuking herself for ever since—then, yes, perhaps he might have contributed just a little.

Instead, though, she said, 'No, you didn't,' desperate to keep him from guessing how cut up she was about breaking up with him. 'It was all through my own stupidity. It had no bearing on anything you said—anything either of us said. It was just one of those unfortunate things.'

He exhaled heavily through his nostrils. 'It isn't my usual policy to end a relationship over the phone like that. I think I just lost patience with you, Sienna.'

So he was going to do it now, like a civilised human being? But how civilised was it tearing someone's heart to shreds!

'Over the phone. By text. Even by carrier pigeon…' She shrugged, uttering a forced little laugh to hide the anguish that was only increasing with every mile they covered, using the very words he'd used when he'd accused her of being difficult to contact that day, endless weeks ago, at the gym. 'What does it matter?' It would still have been like a knife in her heart if he'd dressed it up with roses and champagne! 'Anyway you were right. It was pointless going on as we were.'

'Nevertheless…' That one word, drawn so erratically from him, seemed to emphasise the finality of what he was about to add. 'After all we shared together I had no right treating you like that. Even with a more casual association I would have chosen a much kinder way.'

Was there a kinder way? Some easier option than telling someone who was desperately in love with you that they would never mean a thing to you?

Only kinder to yourself! she thought, biting the inside of her cheek to stop herself from making a complete fool of herself and breaking down in front of him.

He didn't say anything else, and so Sienna sat gazing out of her window at the rows upon rows of houses whizzing by, grateful if only for the silence that delayed their inevitable parting as the houses gave way to offices and shops and the shops became leafy suburbs. Eventually suburbia became open fields bordered by russet and amber hedges, green swathes of pasture grazed by gentle cattle, acres of ploughed earth creating a rich patchwork against harvested gold.

Almost without her realising it Conan pulled off the main highway, bringing the car to a standstill in a leafy lane.

'Shall we get some fresh air?'

She nodded, taking too long to get out, so that he was around her side of the car and offering his hand before she could avoid it. The contact was painfully electric.

Hastily she dragged her fingers out of his and moved towards the riverbank alongside which they were parked. Here a narrow ribbon of water flowed silently beneath shading trees, glistening silver as it twisted and turned, cutting a path across the mellow fields.

They had to talk, he had said. So now he had brought her to this quiet place to make it easier on himself to finish with her. She couldn't bear that. Didn't think she could take the pain of hearing him say it again.

He came to stand beside her, a man who had witnessed such mental and physical brutality by his stepfather that he had closed himself off and was too afraid to love, and yet he had stolen her heart with the depth of tenderness he was capable of.

Taking the initiative, she said quickly, trying to get it out before her voice could crack and betray what she was really feeling, 'There's no need for either of us to add anything to what was said over the phone yesterday. Let's just leave it like that. We can make arrangements for Daisy to see Avril through one of your staff. I'm sure you've got people who can handle these things, or I can always take her there myself. We don't need to stay in touch with each other.'

He dipped his head—rather hesitantly, she felt,

but then it was all part of his act of being kind. And suddenly as the reality of what was happening hit her, it felt as though the earth had stopped spinning. Any second now she'd be slipping off the edge and tumbling down and down into some dark and timeless chasm, and all this pain and misery would mercifully end.

But it didn't. With a violent little shudder, too much of a coward to stand there and take any more of his "kindness", she pulled the brown corduroy jacket she'd draped over her shoulders more closely around her, saying, 'I have to get back to Daisy.' She was already moving back to the car. 'She'll be wondering where I am.'

'Sienna...'

There was such a depth of anguish in his voice that she turned round, saw the same emotion reflected in his eyes. But then he'd been worried sick about Daisy, hadn't he? she told herself painfully. That must surely have left him feeling as battered as she was.

She was leaning against the car as though she needed its support, so petite and desirable beneath her creamy lightweight sweater and jeans that he wanted to take her in his arms and kiss away that harrowed look on her face. But he forced himself to hold back, not sure whether it would do more harm than good. She'd always denied wanting a serious involvement with him, although because of the way she made love—as if no other man existed for her—he'd been presumptuous enough to imagine she was just saying it to save face. But now—because of what happened to Daisy—when there was so much that he needed to say to her—he had been dealt a blow that left him wondering whether in fact she had ever been his.

'Indulge me,' he suggested heavily. 'If only for one last time.' Silently he held out his hand.

Sensing something in his manner that brooked no resistance, Sienna took it this time, following his lead a little way along the riverbank.

Unusually, he seemed to be having some inner struggle with himself, and needing to say something, no matter how trivial, to ease the anguish his silence was only intensifying, she grasped the first thing that came into her head and said, 'Thank you for helping Mum and Dad.' She'd been meaning to express her gratitude ever since last night.

'It was the least I could do,' he said.

'Mum hasn't been able to stop talking about it. About you,' she emphasised poignantly, and then, with a hopeless little glance up at him that seemed to squeeze the life out of her heart, she murmured, 'Sorry about that.'

His smile was jerky. 'As I said...' He brought her hand up, studying their clasped fingers with an almost pained absorption. 'It was the least I could do—especially as it gave me the opportunity to get to know them a little, and to tell you that I think your mother and father are great. They're warm, easygoing and hard-working, and on top of that they're honest—which it seems is more than you've been with them, isn't it, Sienna?' His breath caught before he tagged on, 'Or with me.'

She looked at him quickly, her expression guarded. She thought she'd never seen such bleakness in anyone's eyes. 'What's that supposed to mean?'

He stopped on the way-worn path, pulling her gently round to face him. 'I mean you did a very good job of convincing me that Tim Leicester was nothing more than a caring big brother. But that isn't what your mother very innocently led me to believe.'

The hands that were holding her loosely dropped away as she took a step back. She couldn't understand what it was he was trying to say.

'That week my brother went away... She told me this morning she'd arranged to come over from Spain to see you. But you told her you were joining Niall in Copenhagen and that you weren't going to be around. But you didn't go to Copenhagen, did you, Sienna? And, knowing my brother, he wasn't exactly the type who would have welcomed his wife turning up at one of his friends' stag affairs.'

'What are you saying?' She was shaking her head, her eyes pained, her small features tense. 'And why would she have told you about that anyway?'

His mouth tugged downwards at one corner. 'Quite innocently, as I said. She happened to mention when I passed her in the hospital corridor earlier how you were supposed to be in Spain with her and Barry this week, and that something dreadful always seems to happen when you made plans to go away. I knew she was exaggerating, but she told me then about your trip to Copenhagen, and how it hadn't happened because of Niall's accident. I couldn't help but put two and two together. Work out that you could only have put her off because you were planning to go to this Tim's. Did you love him so much that you couldn't miss out on the opportunity to be with him—even if it meant lying to your mother?' He was looking at her with a painful intensity that seemed to mirror the anguish in her own heart. 'Are you still in love with him, Sienna?'

'No!' Her denial seemed futile now he had the

facts. But why did it matter to him, she thought achingly, when he didn't even love her?

'Then why did you lie to her?' he asked, and then more softly—so softly that it was almost a whisper, 'To *me?*'

In an adjoining field a cow lowed—a lonely sound, almost desolate. As desolate as the fathomless emotion that seemed to be scoring his face.

He was disappointed in her; that was all. Because she had just destroyed all his trust in her that it had taken months—no, years, she thought, agonised—to actually gain.

'I'm sorry.' Conan's voice was hoarse. 'I had no right to ask.' That desolate look about her told him all he needed—yet had dreaded—to know. She was still in love with the man she'd been prepared to wreck her marriage for.

The warmth of her almost broke his resolve to let her go as he placed his hand on her shoulder, and it took every ounce of the calibre he possessed to say, 'Let's get back to the car.'

Sienna turned to go with him, but drew away almost immediately, noticing the glance he gave her before continuing on ahead.

There was a weary slump to his broad shoulders, and his hands were stuffed in his pockets. She was the adulteress. The girl he had always believed she was. And he would walk away always believing the worst about her if she didn't do something to stop him. And she *had* to stop him! Even if it meant going back on every resolution she'd made to protect him from knowing.

'I lied because—' She broke off before he turned round, the admission choking her. Or was it the ravaging anguish she could see on his face? 'Because despite what you think there was no way Tim was ever going to see me with my clothes off. But if I'd let Mum come over, as she was planning to, I knew she might.'

He was moving slowly back to her, his strong features contorted. What on earth was she getting at? He shook his head, bewildered, trying to fathom her out.

She was standing on the path, looking sightlessly towards the river. He could only see her profile, but he thought he had never seen her look more beautiful or more defeated, her lovely face blanched by some painful emotion he could almost feel.

She was small, courageous and proud. Above all else she had a fierce pride and independence he had seldom witnessed in anyone. He would even have said loyalty, if it hadn't been for…

And then it hit him with the sudden weight of a demolition ball thudding into his chest. The way he had found her on that fateful morning. The demure black dress—long-sleeved, high necked—and black leggings hiding her lovely legs even though it had been sweltering outside. He'd thought it was an image she had been trying to cultivate—looking prim to hide her promiscuity. But then he remembered his mother, her face bright and unblemished, wearing those stiff concealing clothes, that same haunted look…

'Niall…*hurt* you?' Shock widened his eyes and Sienna watched his mouth contort with something like disgust and horror through a haze of regretful tears. 'Oh, my love…' Suddenly she was in his arms and he was clasping her to him as though he would protect her from anything that might threaten her. 'Why didn't you tell me?' he rasped. 'Before this? Years ago? Why didn't you say something? *Why?*'

'I couldn't.' The words spilled out on a note of aching remorse, and yet contrarily she felt a strange relief, too, now that he knew. 'He never meant to do it—and he was always so sorry afterwards. He begged me not to tell anyone. More than anyone else,' she murmured, sniffing back tears, 'he didn't want you finding out. I think he wanted to hang on to what little respect he felt you had left for him, and I—I didn't want you to have to face knowing something like that about your own brother.'

'So you kept quiet to safeguard *my* feelings?' Incredulity softened the strong angles of his features as he pulled her closer. 'I would have lynched him,' he growled against the dark pelt of her hair, amazing her with the depth of feeling in his voice. She was still trying to come to terms with the fact that she was in his arms, that he hadn't walked away, that he was holding her and speaking to her as though he really cared. 'How long?' he demanded in a muffled voice, the question seemingly wrenched from his lungs. 'How long had it been going on?'

'I'm not sure. From just after Daisy was born. He couldn't bear to share me with anyone. Not Mum and Dad. Not Tim. Not even with his own daughter. That last time it happened it was because he'd started shrieking at Daisy when she wanted my attention, and when I tried to defend her...' She didn't need to say any more.

Like father—like son, Conan thought, fuming, finding it inconceivable that she—and little Daisy—had suffered so much at the hands of someone she'd loved, and so bravely and silently too. He reproached himself now for the part he had played in compounding her misery, for misjudging her all these years.

'The next day he went off on that stag do, and when Mum said she was coming over I just panicked,' she admitted against the warm strength of his shoulder. 'I didn't want her to see me, or for Dad to know either. It would have upset them too much.' And so she had run to Tim's, not knowing where else to go. Too young still to know how to cope. 'Nothing was visible, so I didn't need to tell him anything except that Niall was away and I'd come up to London for a few days. I made him swear not to tell anyone I'd been to see him. He couldn't understand why, but he went along with it. If he hadn't my parents would have asked questions, and Niall would have gone ballistic if he'd found out. But then he had that accident…'

And she could no more have betrayed his character than she could fly.

She didn't need to say it, Conan thought, caressing her hair, and definitely added loyalty to her list of qualities.

'I wanted Daisy to grow up only thinking the best about her father. Can you understand that?' she queried, looking up at him.

His face, though grave, had less of a bleak look

about it now as he nodded in response. 'Can you ever forgive me?' he breathed.

'For what?' she asked, as though all his accusations and suspicions about her meant nothing.

'For not realising that I was in love with you,' he admitted, recognising that she had just wiped the slate clean of those accusations and suspicions. 'I think I have been for a long time, but I refused to accept what my feelings were trying to tell me because…well, you know why. Because I'd convinced myself I could never be a stepfather to Daisy and that I was doing the right thing in not allowing myself to get too close to either of you. But you were right in what you said that day at the villa. I *was* afraid. It took nearly losing her yesterday—or thinking I was going to lose her—to make me realise just how much I love her and what a complete idiot I've been. I want to take care of her, Sienna, and with you beside me I know I can be the loving father she needs and the one I want to be. I want to take care of you both. Of you all,' he amended, wryly, making her look at him quickly. 'Even that darn dog of yours,' he clarified, because of course he didn't know. 'I love you, Sienna. Will you marry me?' Desperately his eyes searched hers. 'What is it?' he enquired, frowning.

'It isn't just three of us. It's four of us. I'm pregnant,' she told him anxiously. 'I don't know how it could have happened—' hadn't they always used protection? '—but you're going to be a father—big-time. Do you think you can handle that?'

He looked incredulous, but pleasantly shocked, and then his lips began to curve in a way that made his face look lit from within.

'With you and Daisy beside me I can handle anything,' he vowed, placing a tender hand over the as yet unnoticeable little life that was growing inside her. 'Especially such a precious gift as a little brother or sister for our daughter.'

'Are you sure?' she queried uncertainly, even though her heart was singing. She couldn't believe that something so good could come out of something as awful as Daisy's accident.

'I've never been surer of anything in my life,' he admitted deeply, smiling down at her, and then, understanding her fears, he said gently, 'Don't worry, darling. I know you had it rough. So did I. But you and I together are going to put things right. I love you, Sienna. I'm ashamed to say I think I fell in love with you from the moment I saw you standing beside Niall in that register office—though I would never allow myself to admit it. And then that night I danced with you...' He shook his head sharply, as though to clear it of a burden he had carried for a very long time. 'I've never wanted anyone as much as I wanted you that night.'

'Is that why you scarcely said a word to me?' she challenged breathlessly—almost mischievously. 'And made me feel as though you were almost relieved when the dance was finished?'

'Did I?' He made a self-deprecating sound. 'That couldn't have been further from how I was feeling. And what about you, Sienna? How did *you* feel?'

A chilly wind rustled the turning leaves of a silver birch tree that was overhanging the path, penetrating her thin sweater. Discerningly, Conan placed the jacket he'd caught when it had slipped unnoticed off her shoulders earlier around her.

'Scared. Excited. Confused.' She could say it now. 'But on top of all that...' She looked down at her hand, resting on the multi-striped fabric covering his chest, thinking of his values, his conduct, his consideration for others, and his tenderness that was as much a part of him as the hard steel of his body. Now, with eyes that were misty with emotion, she looked up at him and said candidly, 'I felt so...*safe* with you.'

'Oh, my love…' he breathed for the second time, his mouth capturing hers in a kiss that fuelled her desire for him as much as she could feel it fuelling his. When he lifted his head, his eyes seemed to reflect the green-gold fields of an autumn sunset. But there was uncertainty in them too, as huskily he asked, 'Do I take it that's a yes?'

'What do you think?' Sienna said smilingly, brushing a strand of hair away from his face from the teasing wind. But seeing the crease furrowing his forehead, and realising that he was still harbouring doubts, she said simply, and from the bottom of her heart, 'I love you, Conan.'

Clasped against his hard warmth, she thought about all those women who might regret the end of his bachelorhood—even one in particular—but she knew she didn't need to worry. His actions said it all. This man was hers. For eternity.

They stood there in each other's arms until the shadows lengthened over the river and the cool breeze struck up more keenly, scattering bronze and golden leaves around them like sudden handfuls of confetti.

'Let's go home,' Conan murmured deeply, and from his lips the word seemed to mean so very much more. A safe haven. A place where love could grow. A peaceful harbour.

'I am home,' Sienna whispered, tightening her arms around him, and knew that home for them both was where the other one was—and always would be.

* * * * *